I stood at the bow of the boat ... it would be like to be captain o........... .... vessel.

"Ready about!" I squeaked. "Trim the sails! Swab the decks!"

I don't know how long I spent pretending to be sailing. I only know that after a while, I suddenly felt sleepy. Sleepier than I've ever been, in fact. It must have been the fresh sea air I was imagining.

I turned and noticed a nice piece of sailcloth in the bottom of the boat. I decided that a short doze was in order, so I burrowed under the cloth and closed my eyes.

Suddenly, in my dream, a huge wave came up and shook the boat. I was being violently tossed around by the waves (and feeling slightly sick, too). And I heard the ship's bell chiming an odd sound: "BOING-BOING-SCREEE!"

That's when I woke up. I pulled back the sailcloth just enough for me to see that I was moving out of Room 26. Og had been trying to warn me, but I guess the cloth muffled the sound.

It took me a few sleepy moments to realize that I was still in the tall ship, which the boys were carrying to the bus for the trip to Potter's Pond!

READ ALL OF HUMPHREY'S ADVENTURES!

Betty G. Birney

PUFFIN BOOKS
An Imprint of Penguin Group (USA)

PUFFIN BOOKS
Published by the Penguin Group
Penguin Group (USA) LLC
375 Hudson Street
New York, New York 10014

USA • Canada • UK • Ireland • Australia
New Zealand • India • South Africa • China

penguin.com
A Penguin Random House Company

First published in the United States of America by G. P. Putnam's Sons,
an imprint of Penguin Young Readers Group, 2009
Published by Puffin Books, an imprint of Penguin Young Readers Group, 2010

THE LIBRARY OF CONGRESS HAS CATALOGED THE G. P. PUTNAM'S SONS EDITION AS FOLLOWS:
Birney, Betty G. Adventure according to Humphrey / Betty G. Birney. p. cm.
Summary: Humphrey the classroom hamster has adventures going to the library,
learning about the ocean, and sailing across a pond on a sailboat.
ISBN 978-0-399-24731-6 (hc)
[1. Hamsters—Fiction. 2. Schools—Fiction.] I. Title. PZ7.B5229Ad 2009
[Fic]—dc22 2008002347

Puffin Books ISBN 978-0-14-241514-6

Printed in the United States of America

Designed by Katrina Damkoehler

25 27 29 30 28 26 24

With unsqueakable gratitude,
to my adventurous agent, Nancy Gallt

Contents

We Set Sail for the Library

"**G**uess what *I* did this weekend!" Heidi Hopper blurted out one sunny Monday morning.

As usual, my friends in Room 26 of Longfellow School had come back to class with wonderful stories about what they'd done over the weekend.

"Raise-Your-Hand-Heidi, please," said Mrs. Brisbane. Heidi had been better about speaking out of turn lately, but she still slipped up once in a while. After all, she's only human.

When Heidi raised her hand, Mrs. Brisbane asked, "Okay, what did you do this weekend?"

"We went on a hike to a cave and waded through an underground stream," Heidi proudly explained.

I was so amazed, I almost fell off my wheel. (That's what happens when you stop spinning too quickly.) A cave and an underground stream? Now that was an adventure!

"Sounds like quite an adventure," Mrs. Brisbane agreed. Then she noticed all the other hands waving in the air. "It looks as if a lot of you had adventures."

Oh, yes, they had! Lower-Your-Voice-A.J. and Wait-for-the-Bell-Garth had gone bicycling. Miranda Golden (whom I think of as Golden-Miranda because she's an almost perfect human) visited the zoo, where many large and scary animals live. Sit-Still-Seth had gone horseback riding.

"I had Humphrey at *my* house," I-Heard-That-Kirk Chen proudly announced. "We had an amazing time. Right, Richie?"

"What?" asked Repeat-It-Please-Richie Rinaldi.

"With Humphrey. At my house," Kirk repeated.

"Yes!" Richie reached across the aisle and high-fived Kirk.

It was true. I'd had a great weekend at Kirk's. I got to watch TV and listen to people talk. Richie came over, too, but whenever he and Kirk did something FUN-FUN-FUN, like going outside to fly a kite or toss a ball around, they left me behind. I know that small furry creatures don't usually do things like that, but as a classroom hamster who goes home with a different student each weekend, I must admit I sometimes feel a little left out. After all, I'm always ready to help my friends (or even my teacher or principal) solve a problem. It would be nice if they let me share in their adventures, too.

Don't get me wrong. People have been very nice to me. But ever since the day I left Pet-O-Rama and came to Room 26, I've been trying to understand human behavior. It's been interesting . . . but it hasn't been easy.

I'm luckier than Og the Frog, who is the other classroom pet. He doesn't need to be fed as often as I do and usually spends weekends alone in Room 26. He doesn't seem to mind, but then, it's not easy to understand frog behavior, either.

While I was thinking about my friends' adventures, I lost track of what was happening in class for a moment. Mrs. Brisbane was giving us our new vocabulary words for the week and, oh, what words they were! Beautiful words, like *nautical, treasure,* and *squall,* which Mrs. Brisbane said was a violent gust of wind. They were the best vocabulary words I'd heard since I started school back in September, and I quickly jotted them down in the tiny notebook I keep hidden behind the mirror in my cage.

Ms. Mac, the substitute teacher who first brought me to Room 26, gave me the notebook before she moved to far-off Brazil. No one else knew I had it. No one knew that I had learned to read and write, either.

My fellow classmates seemed to enjoy the vocabulary words, too. Kirk, the class clown, shouted out, "Squall! Squall!" Then he took a deep breath, puffed out his cheeks and loudly blew out all the air like a big gust of wind. Stop-Giggling-Gail Morgenstern giggled, but just about everything made her laugh.

The words reminded me of a pirate movie we watched at Kirk's house. Some of the pirates were SCARY-SCARY-SCARY, but it was exciting to see the big ships with their sails flying in the wind. How I'd love to feel the sea breeze ruffling through my fur! And to hear the pirates saying things like, "Avast, matey," and, "Land ho!" I'm not sure what those things mean, but they sound thrilling!

To top it all off, the pirates were fighting with other pirates over buried treasure. I sometimes hide food to save for the future, but the pirates hid gold and silver and shiny jewels. Buried treasure sounds like the most wonderful thing on earth!

I do manage to have adventures of my own, especially when I escape from my cage. I can easily do that because it has a lock-that-doesn't-lock. It looks firmly closed, but I can jiggle it open, get out of my cage to help my friends and return without anyone knowing it. Most of my exploits have been in houses, apartments or in Room 26, but now that I'd been around humans for a while, I longed for bigger adventures.

Lower-Your-Voice-A.J. must have read my mind. (How does he do that?)

"Mrs. Brisbane, can we put Humphrey in his hamster ball?" he yelled out.

"A.J., did I call on you?" Mrs. Brisbane asked.

"Sorry," said A.J., lowering his voice. "But may we, please?"

Our teacher glanced over at my cage. "I guess he would like a break from his cage," she said. Maybe she could read my mind, too.

Although I hadn't had my hamster ball for long, I loved rolling up and down the aisles of Room 26. You can learn a lot from studying the floor of a classroom.

You can find out who is messy (Richie, Mandy) or who is twitchy (Seth, Art). You can even find out who is growing the fastest by seeing whose jeans are a little short (Garth, Sayeh).

That day, I rolled up and down the aisles of Room 26 at a relaxing pace. The good thing is, I can go where I want to unless Mrs. Brisbane stops me. The bad thing is, it's a little hard to hear inside the ball, especially when I'm daydreaming about adventures. Especially adventures on a boat, in the water, on the—

"Ocean," Mrs. Brisbane said, and I heard her quite clearly.

"In the library," she added.

Maybe I didn't hear her clearly after all. I knew that oceans were VERY-VERY-VERY large bodies of water. And I knew that the library was a place where my friends went to get books. In truth, I'd never seen an ocean or a library, even though there was one right down the hall. A library, that is. (There was no ocean at Longfellow School, at least as far as I knew.)

As I rolled up the aisle to hear better, I saw Mrs. Brisbane look at her watch. There's a big clock on the wall, but Mrs. Brisbane still checked her watch a lot.

"It's time to go right now," she announced.

I wasn't sure whether she was going to the ocean or to the library or maybe both places, but I was sure that I wanted to go, too.

"Mr. Fish will be waiting," she added.

Mr. Fish? She *must* have been talking about the ocean.

I speeded up my hamster ball, spinning my way right up to Mrs. Brisbane's feet.

"Me too! Me too!" I squeaked.

Mrs. Brisbane looked down at me. Because my hamster ball is yellow, she looked all yellow, too. Everyone did.

"Not you, Humphrey," she told me. "You'll have to go back to your cage."

There was a loud groan from my classmates. I think every single one of them groaned.

"We can't take Humphrey to the library," Mrs. Brisbane insisted. "What would he do?"

Miranda—dear Golden-Miranda—raised her hand and the teacher called on her.

"He wouldn't hurt anything," she said. "He could stay in his hamster ball."

Wait-for-the-Bell-Garth Tugwell spoke up, too. "He's never been to the library before."

"Very well," said Mrs. Brisbane. "Just keep an eye on him."

And that was it! As Garth picked up my hamster ball, I realized that Og would be left behind. Since he spends a lot of time in water, he'd probably enjoy meeting someone called Mr. Fish, too.

"Sorry you can't come, Og!" I squeaked.

I wasn't sure if he could hear me through the hamster ball. Also, Og doesn't have any ears that I can see, although he seems to hear just fine.

My friends lined up and marched down the hall toward the library.

"You have to be quiet in the library, Humphrey Dumpty," A.J. bellowed. "And you can't check out books without a card."

I was too busy trying to stay upright to figure out what kind of card I needed. I know Garth tried to hold the ball steady, but it was a bumpy trip. Even if I felt a little queasy and uneasy, it was well worth the trouble because the library was a HUGE-HUGE-HUGE room lined with colorful shelves.

I love books, especially the ones that Mrs. Brisbane reads to us. Although she can be serious as a teacher, when she reads, she becomes a new person with all kinds of different voices that make my whiskers wiggle and my fur stand on end!

"Sorry we're late, Mr. Fish," she said. At least I think that's what she said. "We brought along another member of our class," she added. "Humphrey."

Suddenly, I saw a large pair of round eyes surrounded by a large pair of round glasses peering down at me. "So this is the famous Humphrey!" Mr. Fish exclaimed. "Welcome to the library."

"THANKS-THANKS-THANKS," I replied politely, although I know all he heard was SQUEAK-SQUEAK-SQUEAK.

"I'm Mr. Fitch, the librarian," he continued.

So it was *Fitch*, not Fish. But he looked a little bit like a fish with his big round eyes and his large round mouth. Then there was that shirt with the black-and-white stripes and all that blue water behind him. What was all that blue water doing in the library? Was this the ocean after all?

"Humphrey, look at all the fishies!" Lower-Your-Voice-A.J. shouted in his loudest voice. Garth held my hamster ball up, and when I stopped swaying from side to side, I saw lots and lots of blue water filled with lots and lots of fish!

"It's a, uh, naquarium," A.J. explained.

"An *aquarium*," Mr. Fitch corrected him in a kind voice. "A home for fish."

Oh, yes, it was quite a home for fish. There were orange fish, silvery fish, fish with black-and-white stripes like Mr. Fitch's shirt, big fish, little fish and more! There was even a tiny boat lying at the bottom of the aquarium, which started me wondering just whose boat it was and what had happened to the owner. The ship was small—about the right size for a hamster—but it didn't look very seaworthy. What had happened to make it sink? Was it an accident, bad weather (not too likely in the library) or . . . pirates?

"What do you think, Humphrey?" Mr. Fitch asked.

"Eek!" I squeaked. It just slipped out.

Actually, I was thinking that I'd like to be out of the hamster ball so I could see better. But I was lucky to be in the library at all, so it wouldn't be polite to complain.

"Hey, Humphrey!" Kirk leaned down close to the ball. "Why did the fish go the library?"

I knew it was one of Kirk's jokes, but I didn't have an answer, so I just squeaked politely.

"To find some bookworms!" Kirk gleefully answered.

"Oh," I squeaked, even though I wasn't sure that books had worms in them unless they were books *about* worms.

"Okay, folks, gather around," Mr. Fitch told my classmates. "We have a lot to do today."

As my friends sat on the floor, Garth gently set me down near him so I could start rolling my way around the room.

That's when I got a better look at something even more amazing than the fish. Books! Red, blue, green, yellow, pink and purple books. Big, thick books and tall, thin books. Shelves of books all the way to the ceiling. Racks and stacks of books everywhere else. I didn't know there were so many books in the whole wide world, yet here they all were in one big room in Longfellow School. I tried to make a sudden stop as one book caught my attention because of the pirate on the cover. And the pirate flag. It was hard to make out the title from behind the yellow plastic. *Jolly Roger's Guide* . . .

"Attention, please!" Mrs. Brisbane said in her most attention-getting teacher's voice.

I rolled a little closer so I could hear what she was saying.

"A test," she said.

Oh, my, we were going to take a test and I didn't have my little notebook and pencil with me. No one had even mentioned a test before we came to the library.

I still couldn't hear very well, but I did hear Mr. Fitch say, "What floats?"

This didn't sound like a spelling test or math quiz. I rolled to the front of the group, staring up at the aquarium for a closer look.

"Yes, Mandy?" Mr. Fitch said. I couldn't see her, but she must have raised her hand.

"Mr. Fitch, I think we should take Humphrey out of the hamster ball so he can have some fresh air."

My, what a nice girl Mandy was! I used to think her name was Don't-Complain-Mandy Payne, but she hardly ever complained anymore.

"That's a good idea," Mrs. Brisbane said.

"I was thinking about what *my* hamster would like," Mandy replied with pride in her voice. She did have a very fine hamster, thanks to me. And if I was let out of my ball, I could roam freely and get a closer look at all those beautiful books.

"Here," Mr. Fitch said as Kirk opened the ball. "Put him in this."

"This" turned out to be a little square on his desk surrounded by books. Because the desk was lower than the aquarium, I had a good view of what Mr. Fitch was doing.

"Class, Mr. Fitch is going to let us use his tank to do

some tests to figure out what floats and what doesn't—and why," Mrs. Brisbane explained.

I stood up on my hind legs to get a better look. Although the world wasn't yellow anymore, I had absolutely no idea what floats. But I knew something that didn't: that little hamster-sized boat at the bottom of the tank.

If ye be seeking adventure, mateys, the only place to look be the high seas!

From JOLLY ROGER'S GUIDE TO LIFE.
by I.C. Waters

Sink or Swim

~~~~~~

Here is what I learned:

- A wood block is heavier than a plastic bottle cap. Which one floats? Both!
- A piece of aluminum foil isn't nearly as heavy as a block of wood. But when you roll it up into a ball, it drops to the bottom of the water like a small sunken ship.
- A ball of clay sinks like a great big shipwreck.
- When you spread the foil out in the shape of a little boat, it floats! (Though I'm not sure I'd try sailing in it.)
- By golly, when you spread the clay out into a little boat, it floats, too!

I saw it all with my own little hamster eyes, but when Mrs. Brisbane asked why the foil and clay boats floated when the balls didn't, I was squeakless. So were my friends.

"Come on, try a guess, then," Mr. Fitch said in an encouraging voice.

"What was the question again?" asked Pay-Attention-Art Patel.

"Why did the foil and clay boats float, but the balls didn't?" Mrs. Brisbane patiently repeated.

Art shrugged.

"You look like you have an idea," Mr. Fitch said to Speak-Up-Sayeh.

I stood up extra high on my tiptoes to see my shy friend.

"Well," she said in a soft voice, "I think it's because it's spread out and there's more water underneath it to hold the weight."

Leave it to Sayeh to say something clever. I was so glad she wasn't too shy to speak up anymore.

"Bingo!" Mr. Fitch said. Even though I thought Bingo was a dog in a song, I knew he was telling her it was the right answer. It just had to be. There was more to whether something floats or not than just how much it weighs. Once again, I'd learned something new, which is the amazing thing about school.

"Let's try some more stuff," said Heidi, without raising her hand again.

I thought it was a GREAT-GREAT-GREAT idea, but suddenly a loud voice that did not belong to A.J. said, "Excuse me for interrupting. I need to check the temperature."

I recognized that voice right away. It was big. It was bossy. It was, of course, the voice of Mrs. Wright. Who else but Mrs. Wright would be checking the temperature of the library? It wasn't even sick!

"Is something wrong, Mrs. Wright?" the librarian asked.

"I believe the temperature control is not working properly," she said. "And as the new chairperson of the Committee for School Property, I need to keep track."

Mrs. Wright taught physical education at Longfellow School. Thank goodness she didn't teach in Room 26. In physical education, they play all kind of games and sports, which have rules.

Mrs. Wright loved rules.

Mrs. Wright loved her whistle.

Mrs. Wright didn't love me.

"Come on in," Mr. Fitch said.

Mrs. Wright scurried across the room in her puffy white shoes. She headed for the temperature control on the wall. But before she reached it, her puffy white shoes stopped right in their tracks next to the edge of my table.

"What is *it* doing in here?" she asked huffily.

"It?" asked Mr. Fitch. "What's an *it*?"

It was pretty clear what "it" Mrs. Wright was talking about. She was staring right at me.

"The rat," she said.

Mrs. Brisbane quickly corrected her. "Hamster."

"Whatever," Mrs. Wright replied. "He doesn't belong in the library."

Mr. Fitch smiled. "Because he's not a book?"

"Because he's out of his cage. It's unsanitary! What about his *waste*? Where will that go?"

It was very quiet in the library until suddenly Kirk laughed. "She means his *poo*!" he said.

The word *poo* started the rest of the class laughing out loud. Heidi and Gail giggled. Kirk and Richie rolled their eyes and elbowed each other. Even Miranda and Sayeh chuckled. Mr. Fitch bit his lip, while Mrs. Brisbane shook her head.

My poo is just a part of life, but for some reason, it makes children giggle. And it sometimes makes grown-ups nervous. I don't know why, because I keep my poo FAR-FAR-FAR away from my food and everything else in my cage. In my view, you won't find a cleaner animal than a hamster.

Mrs. Brisbane took two steps toward Mrs. Wright. "What waste?" she asked. "I don't see any waste."

"You know," said Mrs. Wright.

"Weren't you here to check the temperature?" asked Mrs. Brisbane, looking Mrs. Wright right in the eyes. "It does feel a little *chilly* in here."

That caught Mrs. Wright off guard. "Really? I thought it was a little warm," she said, hurrying toward the temperature control.

While Mrs. Wright fiddled with the control, Mrs. Brisbane continued talking to us. "Class, we'll be returning to Room 26 now. But we'll be coming back soon because Mr. Fitch will be helping us with the new unit we're beginning," she said. "I'll tell you about it a little later today."

Surprisingly, Sayeh raised her hand. Mrs. Brisbane called on her right away.

"Could we please check out some books?" she asked in her sweet, soft voice.

Mrs. Brisbane and Mr. Fitch exchanged looks. Then they both nodded.

"Okay," said Mr. Fitch. "You've got ten minutes."

Did you ever cross your fingers and HOPE-HOPE-HOPE for something special? I don't actually have fingers, so I closed my eyes, crossed my toes (both sets) and made my wish.

Wishes are funny. Most of the time, they don't come true. Sometimes they come true and later you wish they hadn't! But once in a while, you make a wish and it happens and it's a good thing. That's what happened in the library. I wished that Mrs. Brisbane would pick the pirate book about Jolly Roger. I couldn't check it out because I don't have a library card.

And what do you know—she did!

"YES-YES-YES!" I exclaimed as Garth carried me out in my hamster ball. I was so happy that when I saw Mrs. Wright leaning in over the temperature control as I left, she didn't even worry me.

Not very much, anyway.

My next wish came true after lunch when Mrs. Brisbane began reading that book to us. The full title was *Jolly Roger's Guide to Life,* and it was about a boy and a girl named Violet and Victor who are sent to spend the summer with their mysterious uncle J.R. You can imagine their surprise—and mine—when he turns out to be a pirate called Jolly Roger and he decides to teach them to be pirates, too! Then they set sail to find lost pirate treasure. My fur tingled and I was hanging on every word when the teacher suddenly closed the book.

The other students groaned and I was unsqueakably disappointed until Mrs. Brisbane said she wanted to tell us exciting news.

"Og, did you hear?" I squeaked with delight. "Exciting news."

"BOING!" my neighbor answered in his odd, twangy voice that green frogs like him have, but he didn't sound particularly excited.

"The reason we talked about what floats is that tomorrow, we'll start a project about sailing," she said. "We'll be doing sailing problems in math and science, and then you'll start building your own model sailboats."

My friends murmured excitedly while Mrs. Brisbane paused and then cleared her throat.

"Three weeks from tomorrow, if the weather is good, we'll go to Potter's Pond for a contest to see which of your sailboats can get across the water first. We'll have a picnic and prizes and maybe . . ." Mrs. Brisbane paused again. "Hidden treasure!"

Potter's Pond. Picnic. Prizes. Treasure! My heart pounded at the possibilities, and my classmates' cheers were almost deafening.

"What are the prizes?" Heidi asked.

"Raise-Your-Hand-Heidi," Mrs. Brisbane answered. "The prizes will be a surprise."

My friends groaned again, and I let out a bit of a squeak myself.

By afternoon, Mrs. Brisbane had written the rules for the sailboat contest on the chalkboard.

1. Each student will work with a partner.
2. The boat must be powered by the wind; no batteries or remote controls can be used.
3. All students will be given the same materials for their boats, but they will be allowed to add one item of their choosing (except batteries).
4. Materials will include wood, cardboard, cloth, paint, glue, markers and other art supplies.
5. The first boat to make it from the starting point to the opposite shore of Potter's Pond will win the grand prize for Most Seaworthy.
6. There will be a prize for Most Beautiful Boat.

At the end of the day, my friends were still chattering away about sailboats as they rushed out of class.

Once the coast was clear, I shouted to my neighbor. "Og? Did you hear all that? She said *all students*. I wonder if . . ." I didn't dare finish that thought. Most of the time, I did everything my friends in Room 26 did, like taking tests and learning new things. Sometimes we even had games or parties, and I was right there with the rest of them.

But sometimes, I was left out. Recess. Lunch. PE. Field trips. Still, I could hope.

I was so busy hoping, I didn't realize that it was night-time until the door flew open. The lights came on and a familiar voice said, "Give a cheer, 'cause Aldo's here!"

"Greetings, Aldo!" I answered as he wheeled in his cleaning cart. "Did you hear about our wonderful contest?" As usual, all that came out was SQUEAK-SQUEAK-SQUEAK.

I'm not sure if he understood me, but as he cleaned the room, he noticed the vocabulary words on one chalkboard and the rules for the contest on the other.

"So that's what you're worked up about, Humphrey!" he said with a hearty laugh. "I'd like to be part of that!"

"Me too!" I answered, and Og splashed wildly.

"That gives me a great idea!" Aldo announced.

I waited breathlessly for him to say more. Instead, he started sweeping up the aisles of the classroom. Occasionally, I'd hear him chuckle, but I had no idea what he was thinking.

"Squeak up!" I finally insisted.

"You'll see," Aldo answered. "All in good time."

"What was that all about?" I asked Og after Aldo was gone.

"BOING-BOING!" Og replied. Then he leaped into the water side of his tank. While he was splishing and splashing, I daydreamed about life on the open sea, riding the waves, going up and down and up and down. (I stopped thinking about that when my tummy got a little queasy.) If I had a boat, I could sail the seven seas! I could sail anywhere in the world. I could even sail to far-off Brazil, where Ms. Mac lived.

Ms. Mac! She was my first human friend, and what a friend she was. She was full of life with her bouncy black curls, her big happy smile, her large dark eyes. She was also adventurous. She even took me on a bike ride once, and at night, she liked to play bongo drums. Life with Ms. Mac was THE BEST.

Then she broke my heart when Mrs. Brisbane came back to Room 26 and Ms. Mac left for Brazil. A broken heart hurts a lot. Sure, she sent us letters and pictures, but it wasn't like seeing her every day. At first, I didn't think I'd ever squeak to her again. But by now, my heart wasn't exactly broken. It was just sprained. And I'd be GLAD-GLAD-GLAD if I could see her again.

I don't think Ms. Mac meant to break my heart.

I do think Ms. Mac would be glad to see me again, too.

Funny how a book about pirates gets you thinking about all kinds of crazy things.

Even love.

There be treasures aplenty in the deep, if ye dare look!

From JOLLY ROGER'S GUIDE TO LIFE.
by I.C. Waters

Portrait of a Hamster

BOATS-BOATS-BOATS! Just about all we talked about in Room 26 had to do with boats. There was a math problem about a boat race and a history lesson about the Vikings, who were great sailors and wore impressive hats with horns on them. There were also those lovely vocabulary words.

And there was the story. Every day, Mrs. Brisbane read another exciting chapter from the book. Uncle Jolly Roger, who did seem unusually jolly for a pirate, taught Vic and Vi (that's what he called Victor and Violet) all kinds of wonderful things about sailing. They even had a run-in with a huge whale!

That part of the story gave I-Heard-That-Kirk the chance to tell this joke:

"What do you call a baby whale? A little squirt!" We all chuckled at that.

So, in just a few short days, I went from never thinking about boats to thinking about them all the time. There were so many kinds of wonderful boats, from rowboats you move with oars and muscles to sailboats and tall ships powered by the wind. Then there were motorboats, yachts, tugboats and ferries, which all have engines. And there were the great ships powered by steam. Mrs. Brisbane brought in more books about boats and put up huge posters on the wall.

It would be hard to choose a favorite, but the Chinese junk did catch my eye. That boat isn't junk at all, but a beautiful craft with colorful sails. I could almost feel the sea breeze tickle my whiskers whenever I looked at the picture.

In the evenings, I tried to talk to Og about boats and pirates and treasure, but as soon as I'd bring up the subject, he'd dive into his tank and swim around. Maybe he was trying to tell me that he didn't need a boat to make his way through the water.

I was a little jealous, although I still wouldn't want to be a frog. As nice as Og is, he has googly eyes, green skin and no nice soft fur at all!

I occupied my spare time by drawing pictures of boats in my little notebook. I must admit, my drawing of the SS *Golden Hamster,* complete with a hamster flag, was quite impressive.

On Friday, it was time to find out which of my friends would take me home for the weekend. "Do you have the permission slip, Gail?" Mrs. Brisbane asked.

Gail pulled a slightly crumpled paper out of her pocket. "Here it is!" she said with a giggle.

So I was going home with Gail. Since Gail loved to laugh so much, I was bound to have a fun weekend.

Yippee! I was happy to see that she was also taking home a stack of books about boats.

Gail's mom, Mrs. Morgenstern, came to pick us up. She was a colorful human who wore blue jeans, an orange sweater with red flowers on it, a yellow cap and high red boots. Her hair was in a long braid halfway down her back.

"You know what, Humphrey? I think I'm going to paint you this weekend," she said.

Oh, dear! Mrs. Morgenstern seemed like a nice person, but the thought of being all covered in wet and messy paint didn't sound fun to me.

"It won't be easy," Gail warned her. "He won't stand still."

Mrs. Morgenstern just smiled. "I'll find a way."

As she carried me out of the classroom, I squeaked to Og, "Wish me luck, Oggy boy! I don't know what color I'll be when I come back! Maybe green, like you!"

"BOING-BOING-BOING-BOING!" Og sounded a little upset. Maybe he liked being the only green creature in Room 26.

When we got to the house, instead of painting me, Gail's mom gave me some carrots and gently set my cage on the nightstand in Gail's room.

When we were alone, Gail curled up on her bed with her stack of books.

Suddenly, there was a thundering sound, like a herd of wild horses, coming into the room.

"Humphrey!"

It was Gail's brother, Simon. I'd met him once before when I'd stayed at the house. He was just about as tall as Gail, but she still called him her little brother.

"How's it going, Humphrey? What's new? What's happening? Look at your wheel! Can I feed you? Want out of your cage?"

That was how Simon talked. Fast.

"Simon! Humphrey's *my* class hamster. I'll feed him and take care of him," Gail scolded him.

"Aw, I just wanted to say hi. Hiya, Humphrey!" Then Simon made a funny face, sticking his teeth out and holding his hands up in front of him. "See, I'm a hamster, too."

"You're an idiot," said Gail. "Go away."

"Okay," said Simon. "But I'll be back!"

As he hurried out of the room, Gail let out a big sigh. "My *brother*," she groaned.

She made a brother sound like a very bad thing. And yet, to a hamster who lives alone in a cage with a frog for a neighbor who doesn't even squeak, having a brother seemed like a very nice thing.

I decided to cheer Gail up with a new trick I'd taught myself. Instead of getting on my wheel and spinning it, I lay down on my back underneath it, then reached my paws up and made the wheel spin with my feet.

You'd better believe Stop-Giggling-Gail couldn't stop giggling at that until there was a knock at the door and Gail's mom peeked into the room. "May I come in?"

Mrs. Morgenstern entered, carrying a stack of boxes, with a lot of colorful bags hanging from her arms.

"Guess who went shopping today?" she asked.

I guessed Gail's mom did . . . and I was right. She dumped the boxes and bags on Gail's bed.

"Wait till you see," she said, excitedly opening the boxes. "I got you the cutest outfits! Look at this darling skirt!"

She held up a skirt with blue, pink, yellow and green stripes on it. "It will look great on you."

Gail wrinkled her nose. "But Mom, I like pants for school. I mean, at recess . . ."

"Well, these tights go underneath." Mrs. Morgenstern held up a bright pink pair. She rummaged around in a bag. "I bought three skirts. One with stripes, one with stars and one with flowers."

"But Mom . . . I don't like skirts," Gail repeated.

"Try something new, dear." Mrs. Morgenstern pulled out a fuzzy-looking sweater. "Like this!"

Personally, I like fuzzy things, like hamsters, but Gail ran her hand over the sweater and said it looked itchy.

"Just try it." Gail's mom then reached over and opened a box. "I had another *brilliant* idea today," she announced. "We're going to redo your room!"

Gail blinked hard. "Again?"

"In with the new, out with the old," her mom said with a smile.

"But we just painted it last year," Gail reminded her. "And I like the blue and white stripes."

"*Two* years ago," said her mom. "It's something we can do together. It will be fun! We'll give it a whole new look. You and I could paint a mural. We could make the whole room like the universe with all the planets. Or the whole room could look like the ocean. *Or . . .*"

Gail sighed. "I just got used to my room the way it is."

Mrs. Morgenstern reached out and patted Gail's face. "Honey, try and open up to new things. Change is good!"

Gail didn't answer. She just stared down at her blue bedspread.

Her mom frowned. "Tell you what. I'll leave these samples here and you look at them. And think about a mural, okay? Just think about it."

"Sure, Mom," Gail replied.

Gail didn't seem very excited about painting her room. But I thought it was a much better idea than painting *me*.

After Mrs. Morgenstern left, Gail stared at her striped walls for a while. She pushed the paint samples aside and picked up one of her books. She turned a lot of pages, then suddenly held up her book to my cage.

"Look at this ship, Humphrey," she said.

It was a picture of a lovely sailboat with a billowing white sail.

"I like it!" I squeaked. I know that all Gail heard was SQUEAK-SQUEAK-SQUEAK, but she seemed to understand.

"It's beautiful, isn't it?" she asked.

"YES-YES-YES!" I agreed.

Gail sighed again. "Sometimes, I'd like to sail away on a ship and go far, far away," she said.

"To Brazil!" I said with a squeak. Maybe it was more like a shriek.

"You could come with me," said Gail. Then she went back to her bed and her stack of books.

—·∽·—

Really, Gail's family couldn't have been nicer to me. Great snacks, a great cage clean, no jokes about my poo. Still, I was nervous about being painted.

You see, I'm a Golden Hamster, which means I have very beautiful, glossy golden fur. I never really wanted to be another color. Not red. Not blue. Not green. (I'm not sure there are *any* hamsters in those colors.)

"Humphrey, you didn't eat your carrots," Mrs. Morgenstern said later that night.

I didn't have the heart to tell her that every time I saw the carrots, I thought about being painted orange.

Orange is a very nice color for a sweater or a book or a hat. Even for a pair of socks.

It's not a good color for a hamster, at least in my opinion.

—·∽·—

"Hi, Humphrey! Want to spin on your wheel? Go on, spin it! Want to climb your tree branch? Come on, climb!"

It was morning and Simon was back. As much as I liked Simon, it was hard to keep up with him. Still, he was so excited about everything, I wanted to make him happy, so I hopped on my wheel.

This time, Gail didn't even seem to notice. She just sat on her bed, staring at the pictures of boats in books.

"Out, out," Mrs. Morgenstern said as she came in Gail's room. "I'm here to paint him."

"Oh, Mom," Gail groaned. "Can't we just take a picture?"

"Anyone can do that," her mom answered. "This is more original."

"Can I paint him, too?" Simon asked. "Please?"

Mrs. Morgenstern smiled. "Of course! We'll *all* paint him."

Eek! If they all painted me, I'd end up looking like a rainbow and I'd probably be a soggy mess. Og wouldn't even recognize me when I got back.

"Okay," said Gail, but she didn't sound all that happy about it.

Soon, my cage was on the Morgensterns' kitchen table. Simon, Gail and their mom all sat around with paper and paints and stared at me. Mr. Morgenstern, who seemed like a kind and sensible man, said he had errands to do and hurried out of the house before the painting even began.

"Okay, artists," Mrs. Morgenstern said. "Feel free to paint Humphrey any way you like. He doesn't even have to look like a hamster."

"But I'd prefer to look like a hamster," I squeaked. "A

nice Golden Hamster with lovely fur and no paint at all, thank you very much."

"What's he squeaking about?" Simon asked.

"I don't know, but please hold still, Humphrey," his mom told me.

I tried to hold still, but my whiskers were quivering and my legs were shaking. I closed my eyes, waiting to feel the wet, gloppy paint on my fur. But my fur felt just fine, so after a while I opened my eyes and saw the three Morgensterns putting lots of lovely paint on paper. They weren't painting me at all! They were painting *pictures* of me.

WHEW-WHEW-WHEW! I was so relieved, I hopped on my wheel for a lovely spin.

"Humphrey, hold still!" Gail told me.

"Oops, sorry," I squeaked. I jumped off the wheel and held as still as a lively hamster can. After a few minutes, though, my back leg started itching and my nose started twitching and I had a little cramp in my front paw.

Luckily, Mrs. Morgenstern said, "Well, I think I've captured our little friend. How about you two?"

She held up her painting to show Gail and Simon. I couldn't get a good look at it, but I could see that there wasn't anything golden about her hamster. There was yellow and blue and maybe some purple. "I think this shows the true spirit of Humphrey."

I didn't have time to think about why my true spirit

was yellow, blue and purple because Simon waved his picture right in my face. "Here you are, Humphrey!"

Simon's painting showed an orange blob with all kinds of swirly lines but no hamster that I could see.

Mrs. Morgenstern leaned in to examine the picture closely. "That's very interesting, Simon. Tell me about it."

"It's all squiggly because he was spinning on his wheel. Like this!" Simon jumped out of his chair and began twirling in a circle.

"Perfectly wonderful. I see his eye in the center," said his mother. "You can stop spinning now."

Then she turned to Gail. "Let's see your Humphrey."

Gail held up her paper that showed a perfectly wonderful picture of *me*! I had two ears, two eyes, two front legs and paws, two back legs and paws, some whiskers and lovely golden fur.

"Oh," said Gail's mother.

"It looks like him, doesn't it?" asked Gail.

Mrs. Morgenstern nodded. "Yes, it looks a lot like him. It's just . . ."

Gail seemed upset and not at all giggly. "What's wrong with it?"

"It's fine, honey," her mom said. "I'd just like you to paint what you *feel,* not just what you see. Like Simon's picture—you can feel Humphrey's energy, can't you?"

Actually, Simon's picture made me feel a little queasy, while Gail's picture made me feel very handsome.

Mrs. Morgenstern patted Gail's hand. "It's a very good picture, Gail."

After her mom and brother left, Gail sat and stared at her picture for a while.

"You're such a pretty color, Humphrey. Why would I make you blue?" she asked.

I didn't have an answer, but it was time for me to squeak up! "I LOVE-LOVE-LOVE your picture!" I told her.

I'll never know if she understood me, because the phone rang and Gail ran off to answer it.

The life of a pirate—ah, there be a work of art, me buckos!

From JOLLY ROGER'S GUIDE TO LIFE.
by I.C. Waters

4

A Golden Moment

Later, Gail's best friend, Heidi, came over and the two girls went outside to jump rope. Even in the house, I could hear them chanting:

> *Teddy bear, teddy bear, turn around,*
> *Teddy bear, teddy bear, touch the ground,*
> *Teddy bear, teddy bear, touch your shoe.*
> *Teddy bear, teddy bear, that will do!*

Gail was giggling again, which made me feel GOOD-GOOD-GOOD.

Then I heard Mrs. Morgenstern go outside. "Gail, maybe Heidi can help you decide how to decorate your room," she said.

The giggling stopped. "Later, Mom," Gail answered.

"That sounds like fun," Heidi said. "Paint it pink. Pink with purple curtains and bedspread."

Heidi always had very definite ideas.

"I don't like pink," said Gail. "I like it the way it is."

"We'll talk about it later," Mrs. Morgenstern told them. "Just think about a mural."

Soon the girls were jumping rope again.

I hopped on my wheel and started spinning. Spinning always helps me think. I could tell that Gail was unhappy about changing her room. I hate to see my friends feeling unhappy, so I needed to come up with a Plan.

On the one paw, Gail didn't like change.

On the other paw, her mom wanted to encourage Gail to try something new.

So far, neither of them wanted to give in.

I don't know much about decorating girls' rooms. Personally, I like to be surrounded by soft bedding and tree branches with my wheel and my sleeping hut nearby, but I didn't think Mrs. Morgenstern would go for that.

And I didn't see anything wrong with Gail's room.

Still, I'd been happy when Mr. Brisbane took the cage I liked and added all kinds of fun things. Maybe Gail would be happy with some changes in her room, too.

As I whirled and twirled my wheel, I stared at the paint samples lying on Gail's bed. Maybe there was something Gail would like if she'd only look at them.

The sounds of Heidi and Gail jumping rope drifted in through the open window.

Mabel, Mabel, set the table,
Just as fast as you are able,
Don't forget the salt, vinegar, mustard . . . hot pepper!

Then they counted very fast as I heard the SNAP-SNAP-SNAP of the rope hitting the ground.

33

From the sound of things, they'd be jumping for a while, so I decided to take an unsqueakably big chance and check out those paint colors for myself.

It was easy to swing open the door of my cage. My lock-that-doesn't-lock has never let me down. The hard part of my job was getting from place to place.

Leaping from the nightstand to the bed looked too dangerous, even for me. I'm adventurous, but I like to be safe. I also needed to get to the samples and back to my cage as fast as possible in case someone decided to check up on me. While I was thinking how hard it is for a very small hamster to get around in a human-size world, I noticed the electrical cord leading from a lamp on the nightstand to—well, I couldn't see exactly where, but it was probably plugged in behind the bed.

I am smart enough to know not to fool around with electricity—nibbling on that cord could be a BAD-BAD-BAD mistake—but I figured I could *gently* slide down the cord and leap onto the bed at just the right moment.

I took a deep breath and grabbed the cord. It was smoother than I expected, which meant the ride down was also much faster than I expected.

"Wheee!" I squeaked as I slid down toward the bed and let go. Plop!

I hadn't expected my slide down the cord to pull the lamp over on its side with a loud THUMP! Thank goodness, it didn't break.

I also hadn't planned to land right *on* the stack of

paint samples, but it was lucky that I did, because they all spread out like a beautiful rainbow before me. I never knew there were so many colors, but where to start?

I pulled out sky blue, which was a nice color. The clouds and the sun and the trees all look pretty against the sky. Grass green was nice, too. Flowers look GREAT-GREAT-GREAT against a green backdrop. I wasn't too fond of pink, and neither was Gail. Oh, dear, I wasn't making much progress.

> *Engine, engine number nine,*
> *Coming down Chicago line,*
> *If the train jumps off the track,*
> *Do you want your money back?*

At least Gail and Heidi were still busy.

I pulled out the next sample, which was a golden-brownish-tan. Golden. I held my paw against it, and the paint exactly matched my golden fur! My fur was a beautiful color; everybody said so.

I pulled the sample away from the others so it stood alone right in the middle of the bed.

Just then I heard thundering footsteps and a familiar, "Hiya, Humphrey!"

Simon was coming, and there was no way to get back to the cage before he arrived. I dived under Gail's pillow and crossed my paws, hoping he wouldn't find me there.

It was dark and scary and awfully stuffy under that pillow. I could hear Simon's muffled voice say, "Want to ride in your hamster ball? Humphrey? Hey! Humphrey! Oh, no! Humphrey!" Simon must have noticed that I wasn't in my cage.

Next, I heard the distant sound of footsteps leaving the room. Gasping for air, I crawled out from under the pillow and scurried across the bedspread. Oh, joy, this was my lucky day! The lamp was still lying on its side with the shade on the bed and the base on the night-stand, forming a perfect bridge. I pulled myself up on the shade, scampered across the lamp and gently drop-ped down on the nightstand. I made sure to close the cage door behind me before taking a dive under the bedding.

"He's gone, Mom. He's not in his cage!" Simon shouted as he dragged his mother into Gail's room. I could hear Gail and Heidi coming up behind them, mak-ing worried noises about me.

"Calm down, everybody," Mrs. Morgenstern said. "Let's check out his cage."

Just as they were approaching, I crawled out from under my bedding, trying to look a little sleepy.

"See, Mom, he's gone! He's really gone!" Simon exclaimed.

I yawned, making sure to let out a little squeak.

"There he is, honey," I heard Mrs. Morgenstern say-ing. "He was just hiding!"

Simon shook his head. "No, Mom. He was *gone!*"

Mrs. Morgenstern noticed the lamp and picked it up. "I suppose Humphrey also knocked over the lamp. Is that right, Simon?"

Simon looked truly puzzled. "I don't know. It wasn't me."

I felt a little guilty about tricking Simon, but a hamster's got to do what a hamster's got to do.

Mrs. Morgenstern set the lamp back in place.

"At least it isn't broken." She smiled and turned toward Heidi and Gail. "Let's look at those paint colors now," she said. "Then we can head down to the paint store."

Gail sighed. "Oh, Mom!"

"How cool!" said Heidi, walking toward the bed. "Look at all these great colors."

"But I like blue and white." Gail suddenly stopped and stared. "Oh, but I like *that!*"

I had to strain to see Gail walk to the middle of her bed and pick up one of the paint samples. "It's golden!" she said.

"Yep!" I agreed. It just slipped out because I was thrilled to see Gail smile.

"It's golden like Humphrey," she added.

"It is pretty," said Heidi. "Almost as pretty as pink."

"Fabulous!" said Mrs. Morgenstern. "I never would have thought of gold, but it's brilliant! We could paint a hamster mural on the wall."

"Not a mural, Mom." Gail sounded very definite.

Mrs. Morgenstern sighed. "How about a picture of Humphrey?"

"My picture of Humphrey?" Gail asked.

Gail's mom smiled and nodded. "Your picture."

"Yay, Humphrey!" Simon shrieked.

"Great idea!" I agreed.

When I squeaked, Gail giggled. That was a wonderful sound.

"Let's do it," she said.

I was feeling pretty proud of myself. Gail and her mom both seemed happy. And that made me feel HAPPY-HAPPY-HAPPY, too.

Late that evening, after Heidi had left, I rolled through the kitchen in my hamster ball while Gail and her dad made popcorn, which smelled unsqueakably delicious.

The telephone rang in the next room, and I heard Gail's mom answer it. "Mrs. Brisbane!" she said. "So nice to hear from you!"

I rolled toward the living room to hear what Mrs. Morgenstern was saying.

"Sensational," she said. "Fabulous! I love it!"

Then she listened some more and said, "Yes. Yes. Of course!" She didn't say anything else except, "Okay, good-bye."

Once she was off the phone, I rolled back to the kitchen alongside Gail's mom.

"What did Mrs. Brisbane want?" asked Gail.

"It's a surprise," said Mrs. Morgenstern. "A very nice surprise."

No matter how much Gail and I protested, she wouldn't say any more.

As you can imagine, I was anxious to get back to Room 26 on Monday morning to see just what the nice surprise would be!

~•~

"Og, I thought I was going to be orange and purple when I came back today, but I'm glad that I'm still golden. It's a very good color for a hamster," I told Og when I arrived back on Monday morning.

"BOING!" he answered. "BOING-BOING!"

"Of course, green is the best color for a frog," I quickly added. I didn't want to hurt my friend's feelings.

He hopped up and down in his tank, twanging away. "BOING-BOING-BOING!"

"Hold it down over there," Mrs. Brisbane told us. "We've got to start building our boats for the contest." She turned to the class. "I hope you all spent some time thinking about what kind of boats you'd like to make."

My friends all started talking at once, which is not something Mrs. Brisbane likes to hear.

"Silence!" she said in a firm voice. "Now, I need to know which students are pairing up so I can make a list. Then I'm going to give you some time to get together and plan your boat."

There was a lot of hubbub, but it wasn't long before

the students were sitting in pairs, jabbering away and looking at pictures.

When I was sure no one was looking, I slid my notebook out from my hiding place behind my mirror. I took it into my sleeping hut and stared at my boat drawing. Yep, the SS *Golden Hamster* was the boat for me! Of course, it was only a dream because I didn't have a partner, much less the materials to build a boat. Not only that, my friends kept going to the library to learn more about boats, but I wasn't invited back. (I wonder if Mrs. Wright had something to do with that.)

Once, my friends were in the library a LONG-LONG-LONG time, and when they came back, they were all talking about some fellow named Long John Silver. I could picture someone named John who was very tall, but I'd never seen a silver human—or hamster, for that matter. Oh, and Lower-Your-Voice-A.J. kept shouting out, "Pieces of eight! Pieces of eight!" in a screechy voice. And everyone else would giggle as if he'd said the funniest thing.

I wonder if I'll ever understand humans.

Silver and gold be my favorite colors, me hearties! Bright, shiny silver and gold!
FROM JOLLY ROGER'S GUIDE TO LIFE.
by I.C. Waters

The Trip to Treasure Island

My classmates weren't the only humans acting strangely. One night, instead of saying his usual, "Never fear 'cause Aldo's here," our custodian threw open the door and shouted, "Ahoy there, me hearties!"

I peeked out of my sleeping hut, half expecting to see a real pirate with a patch over his eye and a sack full of doubloons (though I wasn't quite sure what those were). Instead, I saw my old pal, Aldo, staring into my cage.

"Are ye in there, matey?" he asked.

"YES-YES-YES, and you certainly fooled me," I squeaked.

When he threw back his head and laughed, his mustache shook so hard, I thought it might fall off. Luckily, Aldo's mustache is *firmly* attached. "Ye be all right, Jack," he replied, even though he knows perfectly well my name is Humphrey. "I be here to swab the decks. And don't ye be worrying. I'm not a real pirate," he said. "*Not yet,* anyway," he added with a wink.

That comment got my whiskers wiggling, I can tell you! Did he mean he might become a pirate someday?

He didn't explain what he meant, just whistled a

41

merry tune I'd never heard before. After he cleaned the floor and emptied the wastebaskets, he stood in front of my cage and said, "Check this out."

He danced a very happy, bouncy kind of dance as he whistled his tune. When he was finished, he bowed and said, "That's a hornpipe dance. It's named after a musical instrument sailors play. What do you think, Humphrey?"

I was happy he remembered my name again and even happier to be able to squeak the truth. "It was GREAT-GREAT-GREAT!"

"Thanks, matey. Gotta set sail now." With that, he pushed his cleaning cart out of Room 26.

It was very quiet once he was gone. So quiet that I couldn't help remembering the thing he'd said about not being a pirate *yet*. Since Aldo was one of the nicest people I'd ever met, it was hard to think of him as a person who would steal people's treasure, which is what real pirates do. Still, with his fine mustache and excellent hornpipe dancing, I could almost believe he was a pirate.

I couldn't sleep a wink that night, not just because I'm nocturnal, but also because of all the strange goings-on.

"Og, if I could go to the library, maybe I'd understand what everyone is talking about," I told my neighbor.

Og floated in the water side of his tank as if he didn't have a care in the world. I flung open the door to my cage and came a little closer.

"Wouldn't *you* like to know what's going on?" I squeaked loudly, just in case he hadn't heard me before.

He didn't answer at all. He just floated around. Maybe he was sleeping, but who can tell with a frog?

"I was thinking, maybe I should go down there and check things out," I said, raising my voice even more.

Still nothing from Og.

Since I was already out of my cage, I decided to have a little adventure. Aldo would have gone home by now, so the coast would be clear. I slid down the leg of the table and scurried across the floor. The door was closed, sure, but I was able to squeeze under the bottom. After all, I'd done this before!

The hallways of Longfellow School are always a little eerie at night. There are low lights on, and the streetlights shine through some of the windows. But it's odd to be in a school with no children, no teachers and no principal.

It doesn't feel quite right.

I hurried to the library, squeezed under that door—oops, a little tight—and there was that marvelous room filled with books. At first, it was SCARY-SCARY-SCARY because the fish tank had its lights blazing, so it glowed in a way that was pretty, but kind of ghostly. The colorful fish swam around in the bright blue water, and luckily, they didn't look scary at all.

It was cool in the library (maybe Mrs. Wright was right about the temperature being off). I walked up the big aisle between the shelves and the tables and stared up at the tank.

The sunken ship was still there, and I have to admit,

it fascinated me. Whose ship was it? A tiny pirate? A hamsterish fish? Or some creature of the deep I'd never heard of? I crept a little closer to get a better look. There was a series of shelves next to the desk. I found that if I reached up and pulled hard with all my might, I could raise myself from shelf to shelf until I reached the top of the desk.

The light blazing from the fish tank blinded me for a second, and as I stumbled across the desktop, I stepped on something hard and lumpy.

Like magic, a big screen in the front of the room lit up. I scrambled over the bumpy object and—whoa—pictures came up on the screen and music blared. I looked down and realized that I had been standing on a remote control with all kinds of buttons, one of which had turned on a television. But I forgot all about the remote when exciting music began to play. I looked up at the TV screen, and what I saw up there amazed me.

The words on the screen spelled out *Treasure Island*. (I am so glad I learned to read!) There was the sea and a ship and a boy named Jim Hawkins. Before I knew it, I was watching an amazing adventure starring a pirate known as Long John Silver.

Oh, and there was a parrot that squawked, "Pieces of eight! Pieces of eight!" even louder than A.J. had. The bird had a sharp, pointy beak that I would NEVER-NEVER-NEVER want to come into contact with. And there were great big waves rolling up and down, up and down. As I settled down to watch, I accidentally hit another button and the movie started all over again. The words, the music, the parrot. And those waves rolling up and down, up and down until my tummy felt funny.

This time, I didn't wiggle a whisker. I sat quietly and watched the whole movie from beginning to end.

It was one of the best nights I could remember, at least at Longfellow School.

When it was over, I carefully tapped the remote control until the picture went off. Then I dashed back to Room 26, grabbed the cord for the blinds that hangs down next to my table and swung myself back up like I was swinging my way up to the crow's nest of a ship.

A crow's nest is a lookout on the top sail of a ship. I learned that watching *Treasure Island*.

Soon, I was back in my cage, safe and secure.

"Ahoy, Og! Would you like to hear about *Treasure Island*?" I asked my friend.

"BOING-BOING!" he answered.

I took that to be a very big "yes."

꩜

It took me most of the night to tell Og the whole story of the movie I'd seen. If I do say so myself, I did a great job, especially when I screeched, "Pieces of eight! Pieces of eight!"

Whenever I did that, Og responded with an enthusiastic, "BOING-BOING!"

The next morning, once class was under way again, I was dozing away, dreaming about a desert island.

This wasn't just any desert island, because in addi-

45

tion to the swaying palms and the ocean breezes, Ms. Mac was there with me. Oh, and we had such fun, eating dates and nuts and playing in the sand (which I must admit, I like better than water).

In my dream, I heard roaring waves, screeching seagulls, the singing of an ocean breeze. Then there was the sound of Mrs. Brisbane. Maybe I wasn't dreaming anymore. I poked my head out of my sleeping hut.

"Class, I have a big surprise for you," Mrs. Brisbane announced. "I've brought in some helpers to advise you about your boats."

"Whoo-hoo!" A.J. hooted loudly. Garth joined him.

Mrs. Brisbane went to the door, and when she opened it, in came her husband, Bert, and—surprise—Gail's mom!

"Remember, there's a prize for Most Beautiful Boat and a prize for Most Seaworthy," said our teacher. "Mr. Brisbane can advise you on building your boats, and Mrs. Morgenstern is an artist who can help you make them look good."

That news created quite a stir in class. Personally, if I were sailing, I'd want a solid, seaworthy boat. But I also liked the idea of a good-looking craft. Having these two helpers was just the kind of idea a very clever hamster might have come up with!

All of my classmates were buzzing with excitement, except for Gail, who stared down at her desk. I was puzzled. Wasn't she glad her mom was there? I decided to think about it for a while, but I guess I dozed off.

The next time I woke up, Mr. Brisbane was talking. "A boat that floats is a success," he said. "A boat that sinks is not."

I nodded in agreement and then drifted back to sleep. I was awakened again by the sound of Mrs. Morgenstern's voice. "A thing of beauty is a joy forever," she said. "Your job is to make your boat a joyful reflection of who you are!"

Suddenly, I was wide awake. The SS *Golden Hamster* was definitely a joyful reflection of who I was. But would a boat like that actually float?

My friends were already busy drawing and discussing their boats. If only I had a partner to help me build my boat! I stuck my head outside the hut.

"Og, would you like to build a boat with me?" I asked.

"BOING!" he answered, followed by loud splashing.

I guess the idea of a boat is pretty silly to a creature that can swim like Og.

So I watched my fellow classmates make their plans. Mr. Brisbane provided each group with a light wooden hull (the body of the boat), which he had hollowed out because Mrs. Brisbane said it was too dangerous for her students to be carving with knives. He wheeled his chair from table to table, encouraging my friends about their ideas. Mr. Brisbane moves around in a wheelchair after an accident last year, but it hasn't slowed him down one bit.

Mrs. Morgenstern also moved around to each group.

47

She was wearing a green and gold flowered tunic with gold pants tucked into her red boots.

"Color is the key!" she told Seth and Tabitha. "Choose your colors carefully."

"The sail's the thing," Mr. Brisbane told Art and Mandy. "Remember, that's what powers your boat. The Vikings were great sailors. Good choice."

Vikings! My whiskers wiggled with excitement and I strained my neck, hoping for a glimpse of their drawing.

Mrs. Morgenstern moved to the table where Gail was working with Heidi.

"Come on, Gail," she said. "You can be more creative than that! Think color!"

Gail wasn't giggling. She wasn't even smiling.

Kirk, who was almost always joking, was also very serious as he worked on his boat with his friend Richie.

"I've got a great idea," Kirk said as he quickly sketched a drawing. "I know all about boats. We'll make it a tall ship . . . like this!"

My heart thumped a little faster. Tall ships were amazing with MANY-MANY-MANY sails billowing in the wind!

"That's cool." Richie picked up his pencil. "What if we put a thing on the front, a whatchamacallit?"

He started to draw on the paper, but Kirk reached out and stopped Richie's hand. "A figurehead? I don't want to take the chance. It might throw the ship off balance and sink it." Richie stopped drawing, but he didn't look very happy.

"It would look good," he complained.

"Yep," Kirk agreed. "But you want to *win*, right?"

"Sure," Richie said, although he didn't sound completely convinced.

"Hey, Richie, what did the ocean say to the boat?" Kirk asked.

"What?" Richie asked.

"It didn't say anything. It just waved!" Kirk joked, and Richie laughed.

Just then, Mr. Brisbane came to their table. "This is a happy group," he said.

He studied the sketch of the tall ship. "It's a fine-looking craft, boys," he praised them. "Good work."

Kirk and Richie beamed with pride.

"Mr. Brisbane, want to hear a joke?" asked Kirk.

Mr. Brisbane smiled. "Always."

This time, Richie started. "What did the ocean say to the boat?"

"It didn't say anything. It just waved!" Kirk responded. Then he and Richie exploded into laughter.

They were a good team. Or so I thought.

❀

Mrs. Morgenstern's voice rang out. "Now that's what I call original!" She was standing by the table where Sayeh and Miranda were working.

"Gail? Heidi?" she said. "Look at this! Stunning."

Heidi and Gail came over to look at the drawing.

"It's a swan boat," Miranda explained. "I saw one once in a park." She sounded very proud. Speak-Up-Sayeh didn't say anything, but she looked proud, too.

"Okay," said Heidi. "We'll make ours really pretty. Right, Gail?"

Gail didn't answer. She just followed her friend back to the table and stared down at her drawing. I wished I could see it from my cage, but I couldn't.

After Mr. Brisbane and Mrs. Morgenstern left, Mrs. Brisbane pulled her chair to the front of the room, took out my new favorite book and began to read. Uncle Jolly Roger and Vic and Vi finally reached the tropical island where there was supposed to be buried treasure. But when they arrived, they discovered that a band of pirates had gotten there right before them. The very thought of meeting a real pirate gave me the shivers. But it was the good kind of shivers, where you feel happy and scared all at the same time.

When Mrs. Brisbane stopped reading, my friends all begged for more. "I'd like to read another chapter," she said. "But I don't think there's time."

Just then, the bell rang, announcing the end of school. The day had gone so quickly, none of us had noticed. Not even Wait-for-the-Bell-Garth, who was always the first one heading out the door.

<hr>

Usually, after school was finished for the day, I looked forward to Aldo's arrival. It was the high point of my evenings. But that night, I was anxious for Aldo's visit to be over as fast as possible.

For one thing, I liked regular Aldo better than pirate Aldo, despite his hornpipe dance. For another thing, I was still thinking about *Treasure Island* and Long John Silver and Jim Hawkins, the boy who went to sea. I stared out the window until I saw Aldo's car pull out of the parking lot. Then I threw open the door to my cage, slid down the table leg and zoomed across the floor. I was so excited, I almost forgot to tell Og what I was doing. I felt a little guilty having so much fun without him, but I couldn't resist the chance to see that movie again.

I squeezed under the library door and headed straight for the remote control. I punched it and—boom—the monitor lit up. I was all ready to set sail on the open sea.

I was SO-SO-SO surprised when instead of a pirate movie, there was some kind of program about how the human eye works! I guess Mr. Fitch had showed it to some other class. I must admit, I learned a lot about the cornea and the iris and cones and rods.

But believe me, it was nothing—*nothing*—like sailing to Treasure Island.

Keep your eyes open, mateys. There may be rough seas ahead!

From JOLLY ROGER'S GUIDE TO LIFE.
by I.C. Waters

6

Wright Is Wrong

By the time class started the next morning, my mind was spinning as fast as my hamster wheel, thinking about pirates, sailboats and the sailing contest.

Once class began, however, there was too much going on to think about any of those things. The vocabulary test came first. I'd had boats on my mind all week but *not* spelling. I took the test with my friends (sneaking into my sleeping hut to write in my notebook), but I managed to miss three words, including *squall*. For some reason, I thought there was a *w* in there. Like *sprawl*. Or *bawl*.

I must admit, I had a little doze during math period. As soon as that was finished, Mr. Brisbane and Mrs. Morgenstern returned and the sailboat building was in full swing again. I perched near the top of my cage and watched my friends at work.

Oh, what lovely boats they were! The boat Miranda and Sayeh were working on really looked like a graceful swan. It was a sailboat that curved up high on each end. The front part looked like the head of a swan. The back part looked like the tail feathers. The girls were carefully gluing colorful feathers to the sides of the boat. It was quite a sight!

A.J. and Garth designed an impressive sailboat that had a skull-and-crossbones pirate flag (which is called the Jolly Roger, like the uncle in the book Mrs. Brisbane was reading to us).

Tabitha and Seth were building a Chinese junk. It had several sails. The biggest one was red, with a dragon painted on it. And the Viking ship designed by Art and Mandy was beginning to take shape. It was long and low with a square sail with blue and white stripes.

But the sailboat to end all sailboats was the one Kirk and Richie were building. It was still early, but I was already thinking they had a good chance of winning the race. Richie was sanding the hull, and Kirk was working on the sail.

SCRITCH-SCRITCH-SCRITCH! went the sand-paper. Richie was really throwing himself into his work when suddenly Kirk pulled the boat out of his hand.

"Hold it, Richie. You have to sand it evenly. You're taking way too much off this side, see?" Kirk pointed to one side of the boat.

"Okay, okay. You don't have to grab it like that." Richie, who was usually a happy-go-lucky guy, looked grumpier than I'd ever seen him before. "Give it back."

"I'll sand it," said Kirk. "I know how to do it."

He started sanding while Richie glared at him. "I know how to do it, too," he told Kirk.

"Look, Richie, just let me do this. I can practically

53

promise we'll win because I know just what to do," Kirk assured his partner. "My dad and I built one of these last year."

"I can at least *sand* it," Richie protested, but Kirk didn't give in.

"I'll do it," Kirk said. "And we'll get the prize."

Kirk kept sanding. He didn't even seem to notice how upset Richie was.

After a while, Kirk said, "Hey, where do you take a sick boat?"

"Who cares," Richie muttered.

"To the dock!" Kirk replied with a big laugh. "Get it? To the doc!"

Richie didn't answer, and he certainly didn't laugh.

~•~•~

Gail didn't seem to be enjoying the assignment any more than Richie. Heidi painted the hull while Gail was supposed to design the sail. Mrs. Morgenstern loved all of Heidi's ideas.

"Oh, those squiggles look like waves! That's a wonderful theme for the boat," she exclaimed. Then she turned to her daughter. "Gail, why don't you do something like that for the sails?"

Gail didn't smile, and she didn't answer.

Mrs. Morgenstern didn't seem to notice. "Let your mind go wild. Think mermaids! Think seagulls! Think lighthouses!"

I don't believe Gail was thinking about any of those

things. Luckily, Mandy had a question for Mrs. Morgenstern, who moved away from the table.

"Why don't you listen to your mom?" Heidi asked Gail. "If you do what she says, maybe we'll win the prize for Most Beautiful Boat."

Gail stared at the big poster of a sailboat for a very long time.

"See that picture on the wall?" she asked Heidi at last.

"Sure," Heidi answered.

"What does it look like?"

Heidi thought for a moment. "Well, it's a wooden boat with big white sails."

Gail nodded. "And doesn't it look beautiful sailing across the water with those white sails against the blue sky?"

"I guess so," Heidi said.

"I don't think there's anything more peaceful than a sailboat with white sails," Gail explained. "I hate to mess it up with mermaids and seagulls."

"But the contest . . ." Heidi protested.

Gail sighed. "Okay," she said. "I'll try."

She didn't sound as if she meant it.

～◦～

I was GLAD-GLAD-GLAD when Mrs. Brisbane had my friends put their boats away until school was over. After the students left, Mrs. Brisbane stayed to tidy up her desk. It was quiet for the first time all day, so I guess I

55

dozed off. I wasn't asleep for long, though, because I was awakened by a familiar voice, loudly saying, "I think we need to talk about your field trip."

The voice, which belonged to Mrs. Wright, said "field trip" in the same way she might say "bad smell" or "chicken pox."

"Oh, you mean the trip to Potter's Pond?" Mrs. Brisbane asked. Her voice was friendly, but I knew our teacher well enough to know that she was on her guard. With Mrs. Wright, it's always a good idea to be on your guard.

"Yes, I see you filed the proper form, but I did have some questions," Mrs. Wright explained. "And some *concerns.*"

I was concerned that Mrs. Wright was sticking her nose where it didn't belong.

"What concerns?" Mrs. Brisbane asked.

Mrs. Wright leafed through a stack of papers she had in her hand. *"Safety concerns,"* she said. "I need to know that you will have the required number of parent volunteers."

"Of course. That's never a problem with this class," Mrs. Brisbane assured her.

"And all students must have permission slips. No exceptions," Mrs. Wright said in an ominous tone of voice. "Not one."

"Of course," Mrs. Brisbane said.

"I am also concerned about *water safety,*" Mrs. Wright

continued. "I'm not sure whether or not we'll need a lifeguard."

"If we need one, we'll get one," said Mrs. Brisbane. "But the students aren't swimming. They're just sailing boats."

Mrs. Wright shuffled her papers some more. "Yes, well, these are *model* boats, I hope."

I don't think Mrs. Wright saw Mrs. Brisbane roll her eyes, but I did.

"Very small model boats," she answered.

"Yes, yes, I see," said Mrs. Wright. "We'll also have to make sure the students are properly dressed. They will need sweaters. Possibly boots."

Mrs. Brisbane sighed, but Mrs. Wright kept on talking. "Then there's the matter of food. All of the snacks must be on the approved list." She whipped out a piece of paper and handed it to Mrs. Brisbane.

"Mrs. Wright," our teacher said. "I have been taking students on field trips for many, many years and I've never had a problem so far."

Mrs. Wright smiled, but it wasn't a nice smile. *"Of course,"* she said. "But regulations have changed over the years."

I couldn't take it anymore. I just had to squeak up. "Leave her alone!" I shouted. Even if it sounded like SQUEAK-SQUEAK-SQUEAK to her, I figured she could tell I wasn't happy.

"BOING-BOING-BOING!" Og chimed in. I know I

sometimes complain about him, but Og always comes through when you need him.

"Goodness, what's that noise?" Mrs. Wright asked. "Are you sure those animals are all right?"

Mrs. Brisbane ignored that question. "Just give me the forms. I'll make sure they're all filled out."

"Thank you," Mrs. Wright icily replied. "It's for the students' safety, you know."

After Mrs. Wright was gone, Mrs. Brisbane paced around the room making huffing and puffing noises. I understood.

"She is WRONG-WRONG-WRONG!" I told her.

"BOING!" Og agreed.

Mrs. Brisbane stopped pacing in front of my cage. "I shouldn't let her upset me. I think I understand her problem."

I wasn't sure I wanted to understand Mrs. Wright, but I listened politely.

"She teaches games to her students all day long, but *she* never has any fun," she said.

"Yes!" I squeaked. "She's no fun at all!"

Mrs. Brisbane chuckled. "Poor woman. I have an idea of just how to handle her."

She picked up her handbag and left the classroom, still smiling.

I was glad Mrs. Brisbane had an idea. Her ideas are almost always good. I just wished she had told me what it was.

For the rest of the week, my friends worked hard. The boats looked good, but Richie and Gail didn't look any happier.

Principal Morales stopped by Room 26 one afternoon. He was wearing a tie that had little sailboats all over it.

"I've been hearing so much about these boats of yours, I had to come see for myself," he said.

Everyone always sat up straight and paid attention when Mr. Morales came to visit. After all, he was the Most Important Person at Longfellow School. He was also a personal friend of mine.

He took the time to look at each and every boat, and he always had something nice to say.

"They all look seaworthy," he announced when he was finished. "And I should know. When I was your age, my friends and I spent half a summer building a raft. We couldn't wait to sail it on Potter's Pond. I guess I thought we'd be like Huckleberry Finn."

I'm sorry to say I had no idea who Huckleberry Finn was, but I sure wanted to hear what happened.

Mr. Morales continued. "That raft was heavy, and it took six of us to carry it. We slipped the raft into the water, hopped on board, and guess what happened?"

None of my friends seemed to know, so he answered the question himself. "It sank straight down. It's probably still lying at the bottom of the pond today."

Amazingly, he chuckled.

"Oh, no!" Mrs. Brisbane exclaimed.

"It was disappointing," Mr. Morales continued. "But I can assure you, the water in Potter's Pond is very shallow."

"Mrs. Wright will be happy to hear that," Mrs. Brisbane said.

"It's also very muddy. My shoes got so stuck in the sludge, I had to pull my feet out and go back with a shovel to dig them out." He chuckled again. "My mama and papa were not pleased."

Mrs. Brisbane and my classmates laughed, too.

"Just make sure you've got a boat that floats," the principal continued.

On his way to the door, he passed by my cage. "How's it going, Humphrey?" he asked. "Where's your boat?"

"That's what I'd like to know," I squeaked back.

He laughed, so I guess he didn't actually understand what I was saying.

But when I went into my sleeping hut for a nap, I kept picturing a raft lying at the bottom of Potter's Pond, just like the sunken boat in Mr. Fitch's tank.

On Friday, after Mr. Brisbane and Mrs. Morgenstern left, Mrs. Brisbane made a surprising and shocking announcement.

"Class, we were so busy with our boats this week, I forgot to arrange for anyone to take Humphrey home for the weekend."

Whew—that statement took the wind out of my sails! For one thing, my classmates usually *begged* to take me home. For another thing, if nobody took me home, I'd get awfully hungry and thirsty because I can't go without food and water as long as Og can.

"I can't believe we all forgot," Heidi said.

"Raise-Your-Hand-Heidi," Mrs. Brisbane reminded her. "But don't worry. I'll be taking him home with me."

I felt a lot better hearing that. But I felt worse when she said, "I'm afraid there's no time for me to read aloud today. We'll continue with our book on Monday."

No time to read aloud! Just when Uncle Jolly Roger and Vic and Vi were in great danger! I was about to squeak up in protest when the bell rang. Class was over, the school day was over and as soon as Mrs. Brisbane gathered up her jacket and books, we were on our way out of Room 26 for the weekend.

"Farewell, matey," I called to Og.

"BOING-BOING!" he twanged in return. I wonder if that's how frogs say, "Aye-aye."

Life at sea—it's either sink or swim, mateys. Sink or swim.

From JOLLY ROGER'S GUIDE TO LIFE.
by I.C. Waters

61

An Unpleasant Discovery

My friends in Room 26 had been thinking so much about boats, I was relieved to be at the Brisbanes' house, where they always paid a lot of attention to *me*. You can imagine my surprise when they continued to think of nothing but boats all weekend, too!

Mr. Brisbane read about model sailboats, sketched them and worked on them in his garage workshop. Meanwhile, Mrs. Brisbane kept busy writing things on a piece of paper. Every once in a while, she'd stop and chuckle.

When I first met Mrs. Brisbane, she never chuckled. In fact, she hardly ever smiled, because of Mr. Brisbane's automobile accident. But slowly, over time, she regained her sense of humor. Maybe I helped just a little bit. Still, it was unusual for her to sit and chuckle in a room all by herself. People often say and do very strange things in front of me, almost as if I'm invisible.

Finally, Mr. Brisbane came in from the garage. "You're still working on your list?" he asked.

"Yes," she said, chuckling again. "I tell you, this is going to be one fun field trip."

So that was it. She was planning the picnic at Potter's Pond. Oh, what I would give to get a peek at her list! Luckily, the Brisbanes started yawning early, and even though I would have liked to have them set up a nice obstacle course for me to run, I wasn't that sorry to see them go to bed.

You see, I had a Plan. And when a hamster has a Plan, nothing (well, almost nothing) can stand in his way.

I waited until the house was VERY-VERY-VERY quiet. Then I fiddled with my cage door, and as usual, it swung right open. Thank goodness for my lock-that-doesn't-lock!

I was feeling especially adventurous because the only peril I faced at the Brisbanes' house was the possibility of being caught outside my cage. I was willing to take the chance because I had a mission: to find out more about the picnic at Potter's Pond.

I could see that the list was sitting right on Mrs. Brisbane's desk. Of course, before I set out, I had to map my route, just like sailors—and even pirates—do.

I slid down the leg of the low table where my cage sat and scurried across the carpet. It felt nice on my paws, but I couldn't move as fast on it as I can on Aldo's shiny, slippery floors. The desk looked like a mountain to a small hamster like me. However, I knew that where there's a will (and a Plan), there's a way.

Close to the desk, there was a nice cozy chair with a striped blanket draped over it. I grabbed onto the blanket and pulled myself up, paw over paw, then hopped onto the desk. There was Mrs. Brisbane's list, right in front of me.

I was pretty excited until I looked more closely and saw that Mrs. Brisbane had a rectangular paperweight angled on top of the list, blocking part of the writing. I could only make out parts of a few words:

My heart was pounding. *Lun.* Were we studying the lungs, was something going to lunge at us or maybe it was lunch. (That's what I was hoping for!)

Trea made my heart pound a little. It surely meant treasure!

Captai just had to be a captain. Was a real ship captain coming along? Or was it the captain of a pirate ship? Eek!

What about those colors? Were blue and red the color of the jewels in the treasure?

And what on earth was *secret g*? Secret guy? Secret girl? Secret gold? It could be so many things.

I tried moving the paper around so I could read the rest of the words, but it wouldn't budge. I pushed the paperweight with all my might, but I couldn't move it an inch. It must have been made of solid rock! I was still struggling with it when I heard Mr. and Mrs. Brisbane talking. Goodness, I thought they were asleep!

I quickly dived off the desk and slid down the chair cover, which was like a bumpy slide. I landed on the seat, paused to catch my breath, then continued to slide down the leg of the chair. Next, I scurried across the floor to the table. I was moving fast, but I skidded to a stop when I realized I had no idea how to get back up. I certainly couldn't slide *up* the table leg. Still, I'm a clever hamster, so I stayed calm and checked out the area.

I breathed a sigh of relief when I discovered a big stack of magazines on the floor. I carefully climbed up them one by one. However, when I made the leap to the table, my back paws pushed the top magazine off and the whole stack collapsed with a loud thump. I dashed into my cage and pulled the door behind me.

A few seconds later, Mrs. Brisbane came shuffling out of the bedroom, wearing her robe and slippers. "I'll check it out, Bert. I'm sure it's nothing."

She turned on the light and looked around the living room. "Sorry to wake you, Humphrey," she said while I tried to look as innocent as possible. Then she saw the heap of magazines. "Oh, that's what it was." She shook her head. "I hope they didn't scare you."

"Just a little," I squeaked, even though I knew she couldn't understand me.

"I'll straighten these up tomorrow," she said, turning

off the light. As she was close to the bedroom door, I heard her tell Bert, "You're going to have to build me a magazine rack."

"I'll be happy to," he replied. "After the boat race."

〜◦〜

It was quiet for the rest of the night, but I didn't sleep a wink because of what I'd seen on Mrs. Brisbane's list. Especially the mysterious *secret g*.

The boat race at Potter's Pond, the maps and the colorful treasure certainly sounded exciting. With a pirate captain along, it could be scary and even dangerous. Still, the more I thought about it, the more I knew that scary or not, I didn't want to miss that boat race for anything in the world!

〜◦〜

I slept in late on Sunday and awoke revived and refreshed. The Brisbanes were in a happy mood, and so was I. After all, I was going on a treasure hunt soon—or so I hoped.

In the afternoon, Mr. Brisbane brought a model sailboat into the living room. It was a fine-looking craft with a crisp yellow sail and a bright red hull.

"I couldn't resist making a boat of my own," he told Mrs. Brisbane.

"It's great, but only a student can win the prize," she replied.

"I know," Bert said. He set the boat on the table and opened my cage door. "Let's see what kind of a sailor Humphrey would make," he said.

Mrs. Brisbane quickly stacked up books around the edge of the table so I couldn't escape. "I don't think he'll like it one bit," she said.

I couldn't believe that my teacher, who is SMART-SMART-SMART most of the time, could be so wrong! I'd make an incredible sailor—I just knew it.

Mr. Brisbane gently set me in the boat. "See, Humphrey? It's just your size."

Yes, it was *exactly* my size. I felt as if I'd been born to sail in that boat. I stood at the bow (that's the front of the ship) and imagined myself setting sail for a far-off island in search of hidden treasure.

"Looks like he's a born sailor," Mr. Brisbane observed. Now there's a smart man!

"Don't be ridiculous," his wife said. "I wouldn't let Humphrey get within sight of the water."

What an unsqueakable thing to say!

"Why?" Mr. Brisbane asked.

"WHY-WHY-WHY?" I asked, too.

"Because hamsters must never get wet," Mrs. Brisbane explained. "They catch chills easily and get sick or even die. Plus water removes the good oils in a hamster's fur. You really should read up on hamsters the way I have, Bert."

My heart sank to the bottom of my paws. This was worse news than anything Mrs. Wright ever said.

"Guess you're not going to Potter's Pond, my friend," Mr. Brisbane told me.

I felt like I was spinning without my wheel. I felt sick

with disappointment. I felt just about as bad as I did when Ms. Mac left and broke my hamster heart.

"No way," Mrs. Brisbane agreed. "Besides, the poor thing would be terrified."

A lot she knew! She had no idea of the fur-raising adventures I'd had. And I'd hardly ever been terrified, except by large and unfriendly animals, like Miranda's dog, Clem.

Mr. Brisbane put me back in my cage.

"Sorry, Humphrey," he said.

"You think you're sorry," I squeaked. "I'm about the sorriest creature in the world."

They laughed at my squeaking, which hurt my feelings, but I forgave them.

They're only humans, after all.

A landlubber's life is a sorry one, me hearties. I pity the poor wretch who's never known life on the briny deep!

From JOLLY ROGER'S GUIDE TO LIFE.
by I.C. Waters

Batten Down the Hatches

Once I was back in Room 26, I spent a lot of time in my sleeping hut, trying hard not to think about boats. Every once in a while, though, I couldn't resist checking up on my friends' progress.

With Mr. Brisbane's advice and help, holes were drilled, keels were attached, boats were sanded and painted and sails were raised. He seemed especially pleased with the progress Kirk and Richie were making with their tall ship. "Just make sure that those sails don't weigh the boat down," he told them.

"I'm going to test it at home tonight," Kirk said.

After Mr. Brisbane moved on, Richie turned to Kirk. "Maybe *I* could test it at home."

"Have you ever sailed a model boat before?" asked Kirk.

Richie admitted that he hadn't. "But I can tell if it sails or sinks."

"Look, I've done this before with my dad," Kirk explained. "He knows all about boats. He was in the navy!"

"But I haven't done anything," Richie complained.

"Great!" said Kirk. "You'll get a prize and you don't have to do the work. Trust me, we'll win."

I guess Richie couldn't think of anything else to say, but he sure looked miserable. Kirk didn't seem to notice.

"Hey, where do fish sleep?" he suddenly asked.

Richie just stared at Kirk.

"In a *water bed*!" Kirk chuckled. Richie didn't.

Gail didn't look any happier than Richie. Heidi was out sick with a bad cold, so Gail had to work alone. And her mother, who was so encouraging to the other students, continued to insist that she decorate the sail.

"Why can't it be white?" Gail asked.

"That's so unimaginative," Mrs. Morgenstern replied. "Remember how you resisted changing your room? Now you love your golden walls, don't you?"

"Yes, but that's different," Gail answered quietly.

So Gail continued to spend her time working on the hull of the boat. I think she was delaying the time when she had to decorate the sail (or upset her mom if she didn't).

I felt sorry for Richie and Gail, but at least they'd have the chance to sail on Potter's Pond and have a picnic with treasure, while I'd just sit in Room 26 with no one to talk to but a twangy old frog. I know, Og's a nice guy and I wasn't being fair to him, but I was feeling down in the dumps.

Even when Mrs. Brisbane read from *Jolly Roger's Guide to Life,* I wasn't very cheered up.

I thought I couldn't feel any lower, until school was over and Mrs. Wright came in. She was carrying a clipboard and had her shiny whistle around her neck. It's hard to relax around a woman who always wears a whistle!

"Mrs. Brisbane, here are a few more forms you'll need for the field trip," she announced abruptly.

I was surprised to see that Mrs. Brisbane just smiled and said, "Fine. I'll make sure they're taken care of."

"By the deadline," Mrs. Wright snapped back.

"Of course," Mrs. Brisbane replied. "Now, Ruth, I have an idea. To make sure that our field trip is safe and orderly and everything goes smoothly, I was wondering if there was any chance you could come along and help supervise."

I think if I'd been on my wheel, I would have fallen off.

Mrs. Wright looked about as startled as I felt. "Well, I don't know," she said. "I mean . . . yes, it would make sense. Perhaps I can rearrange my schedule that day."

"You'd be a big help," Mrs. Brisbane said (although I didn't agree). "And you'd have a lot of fun."

Mrs. Wright looked even more startled than before.

"Oh, well, of course, that wouldn't be my purpose in being there," she said.

Mrs. Brisbane flashed her a big smile. "Of course not. But it wouldn't hurt to have some fun, would it?"

So that was Mrs. Brisbane's idea! She wanted to help Mrs. Wright have some fun. I didn't think that even a wise teacher could make that happen. The only fun Mrs. Wright had was when she blew her whistle, which wasn't fun for small creatures with sensitive ears like mine.

"Good luck," I muttered as Mrs. Brisbane left the room.

"Good night!" she answered cheerily.

~•~

That evening, I had to listen to the splishing and splashing coming from Og's tank, which only reminded me that he could swim as much as he liked, while I was forbidden to be in water. Ever.

I guess Aldo didn't know that I wouldn't be joining the class at Potter's Pond. He continued to whistle and dance the hornpipe and say things like, "Arrgh," and, "Me hearty."

When he called me a "salty dog," I felt SAD-SAD-SAD, because if there's one thing I'm *not,* it's an unreasonable creature like a dog.

On Thursday night, Aldo said a very strange thing. "Maria has made me a pirate's outfit. She says I look handsome in it!"

Maria was Aldo's very nice wife, and I could hardly believe that she wanted him to be a pirate, too.

"I tell ye, me buckos, this pirate life agrees with me!" he added. Then he pushed his cleaning trolley out of Room 26, turned off the light and closed the door.

"Og?" I squeaked.

I could hear the faint splashing of water. "Og? Do

you think Aldo is going to be a pirate and sail away and we'll never see him again?"

"BOING-BOING-BOING-BOING!" Og responded in a very alarming way.

"I hope not, either," I answered, although I'm usually only guessing what Og is trying to say.

Aldo had left the blinds open, so that the streetlight outside lit up Room 26 and bathed it in a soft glow. The tables were pushed together so the boats were all in a row.

"I'm taking a little walk, Og," I suddenly announced, flinging my cage door open.

I was able to drop down from the table where Og and I live directly onto the table with the boats. It was grand seeing them up close. There was the beautiful swan boat, with real feathers that Sayeh and Miranda brought in. The pirate flag looked wonderfully menacing on the boat Garth and A.J. built. I had nothing but admiration for the colorful Chinese junk that Tabitha and Seth designed. The Viking boat that Art and Mandy created tilted a bit too much to one side, but they still had time to fix it.

The tall ship was missing because Kirk had taken it home to test it.

Gail's boat (and it was practically hers alone, since Heidi had been sick all week) was plain and simple, just like the poster of the classic sailboat on the wall.

My friends were doing a GREAT-GREAT-GREAT job,

and in spite of my own disappointment, I was proud of them. But I suddenly remembered the boat I'd sketched in my notebook: the SS *Golden Hamster* with its impressive hamster flag. None of my friends had even thought of a flag (except the pirate flag on Garth and A.J.'s boat).

I looked around at the piles of art supplies in front of me and picked out a lovely triangle of aluminum foil and a toothpick. I carefully inserted the toothpick in the foil, and what do you know? It looked just like a silvery flag on a flagpole.

I planted it right in front of Gail's boat, sticking it in a mound of modeling clay. It was a way to make my mark and congratulate my friends on their good work, even though they'd never know whose flag it was.

After all, it wasn't their fault I'd be a landlubber forever.

~·~

There's always plenty of time to think after Aldo leaves, and that night, I couldn't help thinking about Kirk and how he was treating Richie. I'd never seen him act that way before. Everybody in Room 26 wanted to win the prize for the race, but my other friends weren't acting like Kirk. What had gotten into him?

Then I started to think about the weekend I'd spent not long ago at Kirk's house. It was a FUN-FUN-FUN place to stay because Kirk's family is nice to visiting hamsters and they all like to laugh, like Kirk does. He has a mom, a dad, an older sister, Krissy, and an older brother, Kevin.

Kirk and Kevin shared a room. They had matching beds, matching lamps and matching desks. Over each desk was a shelf.

On Kirk's shelf, there was a dictionary, a globe, five joke books and a red ribbon tacked to the edge.

On Kevin's shelf, there were three silver trophies, four gold trophies, four plaques and a row of red, blue and gold ribbons. There must have been at least ten of them.

I didn't pay much attention to the difference between the shelves until Kirk pointed it out that Saturday afternoon. He and I were alone in his room. Kevin was out running track, which according to Kirk is a lot like spinning my wheel except you run in a circle on the ground.

"See all those trophies and ribbons, Humphrey?" Kirk asked me. "Those are Kevin's awards for sports. He's great at all sports. Basketball, soccer, track, swimming. Look at them all," he said. "Pretty amazing, aren't they?"

"YES-YES-YES!" I squeaked. I must admit, I was impressed.

Kirk pointed to the lone ribbon on his shelf. "That's the only award I ever got, for honorable mention in the talent show last year. I did a comic routine. I should have gotten a gold."

Since I hadn't been around for the talent show and wasn't even sure what it was, I didn't comment.

"You should see my sister's room," Kirk continued. "I'd show it to you, but she doesn't let me in there. Anyway, she has *two* shelves of awards for good grades and the debating team—that's where people get points for arguing—and drama competitions and speech contests and, I don't know, every time Krissy opens her mouth, she gets an award."

I was still thinking about debating. I don't like arguments one bit, but humans get awards for them!

Kirk flopped down on the bed. "Dad always says I'd better get busy if I'm going to fill up my shelf. Then he says he's just kidding, but I'm not sure. It's just, well, I'm good at being funny, but they don't give awards for that!"

I got an award once for my Halloween costume, but Kirk seemed so upset, I didn't think it was a good time to mention it.

Suddenly, Kirk sat up. "Hey, Humphrey, did you hear about the scarecrow who got the big award . . . for being *outstanding in his field!*" He laughed loudly. "Get it—see, a scarecrow stands in a field. Outstanding in his field!"

"Unsqueakably funny," I said, though I was exaggerating a little.

"I've got a million of them," Kirk said. "Did you hear the story about the spaceship? It was out of this world!"

He chuckled again, and so did I.

Kirk jumped up and stood close to my cage. "Here's one for you, Humphrey. What did the hamster say when he broke his leg? 'Quick! Call a *hambulance*'!"

A hambulance! Now *that* was funny. I hopped on my wheel to show Kirk the joke made me happy.

If I'd had a gold ribbon, I would have given it to him.

Like I said, it was quiet in Room 26. Og never squeaks up, much less tells a joke.

"Og, did you hear the one about the boy who wanted a prize so badly, he'd even hurt his best friend's feelings to win it?" I asked my neighbor.

Og didn't laugh, but that was okay. The situation wasn't one bit funny. And I didn't have any idea how to make things better between Kirk and Richie.

It didn't take long for Gail to notice the flag the next morning. Heidi was back, too, and she asked who had made it. When the girls asked around, no one knew anything about it. (Except me, but nobody asked.)

When Mrs. Morgenstern came over to check on their progress, she asked Gail how she'd decided to decorate the sail.

"Mom, could I make a flag instead?" she asked.

"Fabulous idea!" Mrs. Morgenstern replied. "I love it!"

She seemed pleased, and so did Gail, who went right to work. First she studied nautical flags in one of Mrs. Brisbane's books. It turns out there's a whole language for flags. Boats raise them to send messages to shore or to other boats. Then Gail designed her own series of flags with brightly colored stripes and patterns. I was happy I'd been able to inspire her again.

Mr. Brisbane helped her string them along the side of the mast. Mrs. Morgenstern loved them, and best of all, Gail did, too.

It was a fine boat. They were all fine boats, especially after Mr. Brisbane helped Art and Mandy get their Viking ship to stand up straight.

Kirk looked very pleased when Mr. Brisbane checked out their tall ship.

"It floated perfectly last night," Kirk said. "I knew it would."

Mr. Brisbane was full of praise. After he moved on, Kirk turned to Richie and said, "I think we've pretty much got first prize wrapped up."

"*You've* got first prize wrapped up," Richie snapped. "I'm just a big nobody."

Kirk looked surprised. "Come on, Richie. No one has to know I did all the work. You'll look like a winner."

"But I won't feel like one." Richie quickly got up and sharpened about a million pencils. After a while, Mrs. Brisbane noticed and went over to talk to him.

"Is everything okay?" she asked.

"I guess," he answered.

She tried to get more information out of him, but he just kept sharpening pencils. So she wandered over to Kirk and asked him if everything was all right.

"Yeah. The boat's fantastic—look!" he answered.

"I mean between you and Richie," Mrs. Brisbane said.

"Sure. We make a great team," Kirk said. He sounded as if he meant it.

"Does Kirk really think Richie doesn't mind being left out?" I squeaked to Og.

"BOING," Og answered. He didn't sound very enthusiastic.

Keep an eye on ye enemies, me hearties.
There may be mutiny a-brewing!

FROM JOLLY ROGER'S GUIDE TO LIFE,
by I.C. Waters

Secrets, Secrets Everywhere

~~~~~~

Richie cheered up a little when Mrs. Brisbane announced that I'd be going home with him for the weekend. I was happy, too. I thought maybe we could both get our minds off boats. But once I got to the Rinaldi home, I found out I was WRONG-WRONG-WRONG. In fact, boats were just about all that Richie thought about.

There's always a lot going on at Richie's house with his parents, brothers, sisters, aunts, uncles and cousins hanging out there. They were all there on Saturday—so many kids! Serena and Sarah, Anthony and Alex, George and Josie, Richie and Rita! Late in the afternoon, they all ended up in the bathroom—with me!

I was in my hamster ball, which Richie carefully set on top of a tissue box so I wouldn't roll off.

At first, I was happy that Richie brought me along.

A little later, I wasn't so sure.

"Watch this," said Richie as he turned on the faucets and the tub began to fill with water.

"What's going on?" asked Rita.

George backed away. "I don't want to take a bath! I had one yesterday!"

"I doubt that. Maybe the day before," his sister, Josie, snapped. "Maybe."

"We're not here to take a bath," said Richie. "We're here to see what floats!"

Aha! I realized that Richie was going to show his cousins what Mr. Fitch and Mrs. Brisbane had showed us in the library.

Richie started things off by holding up a penny.

"Float or won't float?" he asked.

"Won't!" his cousins shouted in unison.

The penny sank to the bottom of the tub.

Next, George took a pencil out of his pocket. "Float or won't float?"

"Will!" Rita, Serena and Sarah agreed.

"Won't!" Alex, Anthony and Josie agreed.

The pencil floated beautifully. All it needed was a sail to look just like a sailboat.

The cousins soon scattered all over the house and returned with more things to test. They tried a peppermint stick (sank), a flip-flop (floated), a leaf (floated until it got soggy and sank) and a seashell (sank). A plastic cup did something very surprising. It floated on its side until it was three-quarters full of water, then it tipped up and floated upright.

Finally, a teddy bear floated on his back with a big happy smile on his face. I guess it's okay for furry teddy bears to get wet, unlike furry hamsters.

Then George and Anthony got into a splashing fight. George's dad looked in to see what was going on.

"It's a science experiment," Richie told him.

"Anything that can get George to the bathtub is fine with me," he said. "Just clean up the mess when you're finished."

It was fun to watch all the splashing until Alex grabbed the hamster ball and said, "What about this? Will it float?"

"NO-NO-NO!" I squeaked. I didn't know if the ball would float or not, but I knew that I didn't want to get wet! And even though the plastic would protect me from the water, those air holes were sure to let water in. When I'd wished for an adventure on the water, this wasn't what I had in mind!

Alex was carrying me toward the tub as I shrieked, "Stop him! I shouldn't get wet!"

I wasn't sure if anyone could hear me with all that plastic around me.

He held the ball over the water. I took a deep breath and squeaked, "Eeeeeeek!"

At that point, my friend Richie grabbed the ball out of Alex's hand. "Not with Humphrey in it, you dodo."

Richie opened the ball, took me out and handed the ball back to his cousin. "Here," he said.

Alex dropped my hamster ball into the tub, where it bobbed up and down on the water, floating along.

My heart was pounding, but I was GLAD-GLAD-GLAD I wasn't inside.

Richie put me back in my cage, where I burrowed into my sleeping hut for a long, dry nap.

On Sunday afternoon, Richie cleaned my cage. He did an excellent job. While he was changing my water, his mom brought in the phone and said he had a call.

"Hello?" Richie said. "Oh . . . Kirk."

He sure didn't seem happy to hear from his partner.

"Okay. Okay. Okay." That's all I heard. I couldn't hear what Kirk said, but Richie told me after he said good-bye.

"Dumb old Kirk. He took the boat home again and wanted to tell me it sailed really great," Richie explained. "What a jerk. Kirk the jerk."

Then he unexpectedly slipped me in his pocket. It was dark in there, but I could make out a couple of dried-up raisins and half a stick of gum stuck to the cloth. Luckily, I was only there for a few seconds.

Richie went into the bathroom, locked the door, took me out of his pocket and set me in an empty soap dish. I was a little nervous when he started filling the bathtub with water, especially after the experiments from the day before.

"Don't worry, Humphrey. You're not getting a bath," Richie assured me. "I just want to show you something. It's a secret."

Once the tub was full, he showed me a strange-looking boat. "This is my remote-controlled submarine. Pretty cool, isn't it?"

The submarine was a very sleek boat, nothing like the sailboats we'd been studying. It was completely gray and had no sails at all—just a tower-like thing coming up out of the middle.

"Here's the periscope." Richie pointed to a long, narrow tube coming out of the tower. "When you're underwater, you can use it to see what's on top of the water."

Amazing.

"In real submarines, people can live underwater for weeks. Even months. They can sneak up on enemies because no one even knows they're there," Richie said.

After he put the submarine in the tub, he used a remote control—like the one for Mr. Fitch's television—to make it move through the water.

"I can control when it goes up and when it goes down," he explained. "See?"

Using the controls in his hands, he made the submarine dive down until it was completely underwater. It glided silently across the bottom of the tub.

"Now, watch this," he said.

I watched carefully as he pushed some buttons, and suddenly, the submarine glided up to the surface of the water.

"That's GREAT-GREAT-GREAT," I squeaked happily.

My classmates are so clever!

But my little hamster heart sank almost to my stomach when Richie said, "I'm going to take this submarine to Potter's Pond for the boat race."

"That's against the rules," I squeaked.

"Kirk thinks he's so smart," Richie muttered. The submarine dived to the bottom of the tub. "I'll hide it in my backpack. While the race is on, I'll sneak to the sidelines, slip the submarine in the water, then bring it up right next to his stupid tall ship. Just to show him I can handle a boat, too."

"Something could go wrong! What if the submarine hits the boat?" I tried to warn him, but it was no use.

"I'll probably get in trouble," Richie admitted. "But I don't want the stupid prize, anyway."

My mind was racing. If I could get my paws on that controller, maybe I could stop him. But Richie put the submarine and the device in a cabinet way up high. I could see there was no way a small hamster could reach it.

I've helped a lot of my friends on a lot of my weekend visits, but there was no way I could change Richie's mind.

"It'll be our little secret," he told me.

It wasn't a secret I wanted to keep. At least I wouldn't be there to see it.

"Good news, class," Mrs. Brisbane announced on Monday. "The weather tomorrow should be picture-perfect, so the trip to Potter's Pond is on."

My friends gave a cheer. Even though the picnic was *off* for me, I managed a celebratory squeak.

I felt terrible for Mrs. Brisbane. She'd planned everything so well, but things weren't going to go according to her plan unless I came up with a bright idea to stop Richie.

Everyone was excited about the picnic the next day, but they were perfectly quiet when Mrs. Brisbane read the final chapter to the Uncle Jolly Roger book. Vic and Vi helped their uncle scare off the pirates (with the help of a very loud whistle—can you believe it?). And then, to the children's surprise, they set sail with the treasure to return it to the real owners. It turns out that Uncle Jolly Roger was a *good* pirate!

Richie was a good guy, too. And good guys don't do bad things, do they? Well, maybe sometimes they do.

I needed a Plan. But in order to have a Plan, I needed research. Mrs. Brisbane talked about research from time to time, and I figured out it meant learning more about a subject. When students had to do research, they usually went to the library. So I decided to undertake a little research project of my own.

First, I had to wait for Aldo to finish cleaning the room. He was very cheery that night, whistling the hornpipe song and dancing around with the broom.

"Well, me buckos, tomorrow I set sail," he said. "I hope your friends don't get attacked by pirates."

The thought of pirates attacking anyone, especially my friends, made my whiskers twitch, but Aldo let out a jolly laugh.

~~~

I waited a long time after Aldo left to make sure he'd left Longfellow School for the night. Then I told Og about my mission, slipped out of my cage, slid under the door and headed toward the library. The hallways didn't seem so eerie anymore. I guess I was getting used to my night-time journeys.

Once I squeezed under the door of the library, I stopped to catch my breath and look around. The fish tank was glowing, thank goodness, because I needed the light. I headed straight for the remote control. If I could figure out how it worked, maybe I could figure out how to make Richie's remote *not* work. I scrambled up the stair-like shelves and scampered across the desk to the remote control.

Research can be HARD-HARD-HARD, as I found out that night, but I learned a lot. First of all, remotes don't have cords that you can plug and unplug, like televisions and irons and other objects humans use.

Second of all, those buttons do some very strange things besides turning a television on and off. I found the On/Off button and up on the screen, I saw a group of children walking down a sidewalk. When I pushed the next button, the children started walking backward, which was pretty funny. I hate to admit, I spent quite a bit of time making those kids walk forward and then backward.

Then it was time to get on with my research. One button turned the sound on and off, and others made the picture do all kinds of strange things, like change color and get squiggly lines. None of the buttons made the remote stop except the On/Off button.

There had to be something else that made the remote work. I checked more carefully and found a little compartment in the back. When I jiggled it open, two batteries rolled out. The batteries were the secret! Sure enough, when the batteries weren't in the remote, no matter how many times I pushed the On/Off button, nothing happened.

If I could take out the batteries, I could put Richie's remote out of action. So the next morning, all I had to do was (a) get into his backpack, (b) find his remote and (c) take out the batteries . . . (d) without anyone noticing!

That was a tall order for a small hamster, but I vowed to give it my best shot. I could only cross my paws and hope that my friends would leave for Potter's Pond after morning recess and not first thing in the morning.

But before that, I needed to get Mr. Fitch's batteries back in their little compartment. Let me tell you, taking batteries out is a lot easier than putting them in. It took me four—no, five—tries before the screen lit up and those children walked down the sidewalk again.

Whew! I couldn't resist hitting the button that took the movie back to the beginning, and I saw its title: *Safety First*. It explained how children should cross a street safely, and oh, it was a very frightening sight! The children learned how to look both ways before crossing a street, how to wait for a kindly crossing guard to stop traffic with a sign and how to press a button on a pole and wait until a picture of a person walking lit up. Those kids were very good at being safe.

But I couldn't help thinking about how unsafe a little hamster would be out on the sidewalk. All those big feet clomping along and huge cars whizzing by! The kindly crossing guard probably wouldn't be able to see me, and there was NO-NO-NO way a creature of my size could reach up that pole and press the button for the Walk light.

Not only were hamsters in danger around water, we were unsafe out on the sidewalk. I hit the On/Off button and dashed for the door. But as anxious as I was to get back to Room 26, I was stopped in my tracks by the sight of something under Mr. Fitch's desk.

Being a naturally curious creature, I looked more closely. I was amazed at what I saw. It was a genuine pirate hat: big and black with a broad brim, right there in the library!

Had a pirate been here and left it behind? Was Mr. Fitch secretly a pirate?

"Shiver me timbers!" I squeaked, and I dashed out of the library and back to the safety of Room 26 as fast as my small legs could carry me.

Be careful, all ye treasure seekers. You might find more than ye bargained for!
From JOLLY ROGER'S GUIDE TO LIFE,
by I.C. Waters

Anchors Aweigh

BOING-BOING-BOING!"

That was Og's reaction when I told him about my experience in the library. Even though I didn't think he understood what a remote control is, he got the general idea, and when I told him about the pirate hat, he splashed so madly, I was in danger of getting soaked right there on our table.

After Og settled down a little, I knew I should get some sleep so I'd be alert and ready if I had a chance to get into Richie's backpack the next morning.

Still, I couldn't resist taking one more look at the beautiful boats my classmates worked so hard on. They looked seaworthy enough, thanks to Mr. Brisbane's advice. And they were beautiful, with Mrs. Morgenstern's help. Gail's nautical flags were bright and colorful. So were the sails on the Chinese junk. But in the end, my favorite was the tall ship, because it looked as if it really could sail FAR-FAR-FAR away.

Standing in front of this wonderful boat was about as close as I was going to come to the adventure I'd been wishing for. I longed to be a little bit closer. It couldn't hurt if I just crawled into the boat and pretended to sail for a minute or two, could it?

I stood at the bow of the boat and tried to imagine what it would be like to be captain of such a fine vessel.

"Ready about!" I squeaked. "Trim the sails! Swab the decks!"

I admit, I didn't know what all those things meant, but I'd heard them in books and movies.

"Lower the boom! Batten down the hatches!" It felt good to say those things.

"Heave-ho!" I shouted. I heard Og splashing in the background, but I was hardly aware that I was in Room 26.

I don't know how long I spent pretending to be sailing. I only know that after a while, I suddenly felt sleepy. Sleepier than I've ever been, in fact. It must have been the fresh sea air I was imagining.

I turned and noticed a nice piece of sailcloth in the bottom of the boat. I decided that a short doze was in order, so I burrowed under the cloth and closed my eyes. I guess I was dreaming because I could see the boat gliding across a silver sea, and then the dream turned SCARY-SCARY-SCARY because I saw a pirate ship approaching. And there were real live pirates on board, wearing shiny red jackets with gold buttons and big pirate hats.

"Turn back!" I yelled. "Trim the sails! Flibber the gibbet!"

I wasn't making much sense, but the words sounded

pretty good. Suddenly, in my dream, a huge wave came up and shook the boat. I was being violently tossed around by the waves (and feeling slightly sick, too). And I heard the ship's bell chiming an odd sound: "BOING-BOING-SCREEE!"

That's when I woke up. I pulled back the sailcloth just enough for me to see that I was moving out of Room 26. Og had been trying to warn me, but I guess the cloth muffled the sound.

I heard voices.

"Can't I at least carry it?" Richie begged.

"Better if I do it," Kirk replied. "Trust me."

It took me a few sleepy moments to realize that I was still in the tall ship, which the boys were carrying to the bus for the trip to Potter's Pond! I was about to squeak up in protest when I thought that at last, I had an opportunity for real adventure. I was going to Potter's Pond! And maybe, just maybe, I'd still have the chance to disable Richie's remote.

"Nice, breezy day for sailing," I heard Mr. Brisbane say.

I burrowed back under the cloth as my friends chattered away. Soon I felt the vibration of the bus.

"Everybody, find a seat." That, I knew, was the familiar voice of Miss Victoria, the bus driver.

SCREEEEEECH!

It's a good thing I was already lying down in the bottom of the boat or I would have surely been knocked over by the horrible sound of Mrs. Wright's whistle. If that was her idea of fun, I was already sorry I'd stowed away.

"I am missing one permission slip," she announced. "This bus cannot leave the school without it. Is Richie Rinaldi on the bus?"

"What?" Repeat-It-Please-Richie's muffled voice replied.

"Richie, I must have your permission slip or you will have to leave the bus," Mrs. Wright told him.

It was mostly quiet—except for the shuffling of some paper. He must have been rummaging around in his backpack. Backpack! That's probably where he had the remote control, too.

"I've got it!" Richie said.

A few minutes later, the bus rumbled away from the school, on its way to Potter's Pond . . . with me on board!

My friends were kind of noisy—they always are on the bus. Then I heard Mrs. Brisbane say, "Mrs. Wright, I think it would be fun if you led us in some songs."

Mrs. Wright sounded surprised. "Me? Well, I could, I suppose. If you'd like me to."

"I'd like you to," Mrs. Brisbane replied.

I braced myself for the whistle. SCREEEECH!

"All right, class. Everybody sing!" Mrs. Wright commanded my friends.

Everybody sang—probably to avoid hearing the whistle again—as Mrs. Wright led them in a song that was VERY-VERY-VERY noisy!

If you're happy and you know it
Clap your hands.

And everyone clapped!

If you're happy and you know it
Clap your hands.

More loud clapping.

If you're happy and you know it
And you really want to show it,
If you're happy and you know it
Clap your hands.

Thunderous clapping!

I clapped my paws, too. Then I remembered Richie's backpack again. Was there any way for me to slip out of the boat and into the backpack without anyone noticing?

Mrs. Wright blew her whistle again. SCREEEECH!

"Keep it going, students!" she barked. And they did.

If you're happy and you know it
Stamp your feet.

The students stamped in a way that would have gotten them in trouble if they were in class and not on the bus.

I decided this was *not* the time to escape from the boat.

> *If you're happy and you know it*
> *Stamp your feet.*

Even louder stamping. I am surprised the floor of the bus didn't collapse with all that stamping, but my friends—and Mrs. Wright—were having so much fun, they kept on going. They added a verse where everyone shouted, "We are!" and then another where everyone did all three things: clapping, stamping and shouting, "We are!"

As much fun as everyone was having, I was feeling quite miserable. I wanted to get to that remote control and stop Richie from getting in trouble. And I wanted to warn my friends that they might meet up with some unfriendly pirates.

But I also knew that if Mrs. Wright discovered a small, unsanitary hamster on the bus, it would ruin *everything*. So I listened to the happy commotion and stayed put.

Suddenly, the rumbling of the bus stopped.

"Let's thank Mrs. Wright for making this trip so much fun," I heard Mrs. Brisbane say.

My friends all cheered loudly, which must have made Mrs. Wright feel good.

"All out for Potter's Pond," Mrs. Brisbane announced.

There was so much noise, so much bumping and thumping, so much confusion that all I could do was lie low, hang on tightly and hope for the best.

It took a while to get everyone lined up. I heard the voices of some of the parents, like Heidi's mom, Miranda's dad, Gail's mom, Art's mom and Sayeh's dad. This was some big party!

At last Mrs. Brisbane made the big announcement. "Boys and girls, on the count of three, set your boats on the water," she said.

"One . . . two . . . three!"

SCREEEECH. Somehow, I wasn't surprised that Mrs. Wright blew her whistle to start the race.

There was a big bump, a bigger thump and then—oh, my—I felt myself floating for the first time in my life. It felt like I was riding on a cloud.

My classmates screamed, "GO-GO-GO!" Once I was used to the feeling of drifting on water, I pushed the cloth back a little and peeked over the side of the boat.

What a sight! Ahead of me, rippling blue water. In the distance, a leafy green shoreline. On either side of me, my friends' boats, now afloat. Above me, sails gently rippling. I ventured up to the bow of the ship and felt the soft breeze against my fur. It was glorious!

On the shore, my classmates were lined up on both sides of the pond, cheering their boats on.

The ship was sailing so smoothly, I relaxed a little.

I glanced behind me just in time to see the delicate swan boat that Sayeh and Miranda had worked so hard on rapidly sink out of view. There were moans and groans from the shore, and I groaned a little, too.

The pirate ship was the next boat to go under. There

were more groans, but others cheered for the remaining boats.

I was getting nervous. Was my boat going to sink, too? My tummy did a FLIP-FLOP-FLIP. But my tall ship seemed to glide effortlessly through the water. I guess Kirk really *did* know what he was doing.

The Chinese junk and the flag-filled sailboat were still on the water but lagging far behind me. Even farther back was the tip of the Viking ship, which was sinking rapidly.

"Go!" my friends chanted. "Go!"

Then suddenly, I heard Lower-Your-Voice-A.J.'s loud voice booming, "Humphrey Dumpty's on that boat!"

There was a gasp, and Mrs. Brisbane shouted, "It *is* Humphrey! How did he get on that boat? Kirk? Richie?"

In the distance, I heard Kirk say, "I don't know." He sounded confused. "I didn't see him."

"Somebody's going to be in big trouble." Mrs. Brisbane didn't sound happy at all.

If Mrs. Brisbane was right about hamsters getting wet, I was already in big trouble, but as the boat glided through the water, I felt freer than I've ever been. This was my greatest adventure yet, and I decided to enjoy it.

Pillaging and plundering can be a bit wearing, but there be no better place to live than on the open sea!

From JOLLY ROGER'S GUIDE TO LIFE,
by I.C. Waters

All at Sea

hoy, mateys!" I squeaked toward shore, even though
I knew no one could hear me. Then in my best pirate voice, I added, "Arrgh!"

My friends were cheering wildly when suddenly, out
of the corner of my eye, I saw something dark in the
water. For an instant, I remembered a report on sharks
that Art had read to the class. Eek! Then I recognized the
shape of Richie's submarine gliding through the water,
heading straight for me!

Suddenly, the submarine began to surface. Richie had
said it was supposed to come up next to the boat, but it
was heading directly for it. I wasn't the only one who
noticed as I heard voices, voices, everywhere!

"It's a submarine!"

"Where'd that come from?"

"Richie's in the bushes and he has a remote control!"

"It's going to hit the boat!"

EEK-EEK-EEK!

That's when I heard Repeat-It-Please-Richie's voice.
"What?" he asked.

A.J.'s voice was loud and clear. "It's going to hit the boat, and Humphrey's on it!"

"Humphrey?!" Richie sounded shocked.

"Do something, Richie!" Mandy screamed.

"I'm trying!" he shouted back.

I could see people running around onshore, but I was hanging on for dear life and didn't have time to pay much attention to them. Just then, the submarine hit and the sailboat tilted sharply to one side. Luckily, I managed to hang on to the bow of the boat or else I would have slid into the water to, well, certain disaster.

I'm sure Richie didn't mean to hit the ship. Maybe he wasn't as good at handling a submarine as he'd thought.

Onshore, my friends were in a panic. "Save him! Save Humphrey!" they screamed.

"Save me!" I squeaked as the boat rocked and rolled.

"Whose sub is it?" Mrs. Brisbane called. I'd never heard her voice so alarmed.

"Mine," Richie answered. "I'm backing it away."

SCREEEEECH! I don't know what Mrs. Wright thought the whistle would do to help me, but she blew it over and over again.

And then, the boat tipped all the way over on its side, the sails floating next to it in the water.

My friends all shrieked, "Humphrey!"

"Eeek!" I squeaked. I suddenly wished Og was around to help me out.

I hung on to the side for dear life, but the water was

getting closer and, believe me, it was too close for comfort.

"We're going down!" I squeaked, although I was actually the only one going down.

I remembered Mr. Morales saying the pond was shallow, but for a hamster it would surely be DEEP-DEEP-DEEP. I tried not to think about the little sunken ship at the bottom of Mr. Fitch's fish tank.

I also recalled Mrs. Brisbane's warning about hamsters getting wet. I wasn't sure whether I could swim or not, but I didn't want to find out.

Just then, I saw the long periscope of Richie's submarine right next to me. I took a deep breath and leaped across the water to grab hold of it. (All those hours of jumping on my wheel and spinning have certainly paid off.)

"Now he's hanging on to the periscope!" That was A.J. shouting. "Look!"

There were cheers from the shore, but I wasn't about to cheer until I reached dry land.

I was clinging to the periscope for dear life when the beautiful tall ship dropped down below the edge of the water.

Mrs. Brisbane shouted at Richie, "Can you bring him in safely?"

"I can do it," he answered.

No hamster ever hung on to anything as tightly as I hung on to that periscope. The water was only inches below me. I wouldn't have minded being a googly-eyed green frog with no fur at all, at least for a few minutes. But soon, the submarine glided toward shore.

Without hesitation, Richie and Kirk both waded out to rescue me. They didn't even worry about their clothes getting wet. Luckily, Mr. Morales was right. The water in Potter's Pond was shallow—at least to humans.

"Hurry!" said Kirk. "It's going to sink."

"Okay, but watch it," Richie replied as they approached the submarine. "We don't want to splash water on Humphrey."

Richie gently plucked me off the periscope and held me in his cupped hands.

"Sorry, Humphrey," he said softly. "I'm so sorry."

I was shivering as he carefully carried me to shore and handed me to Mrs. Brisbane.

"You're shaking," she said, and she was right.

She opened the lid of a small woven basket and took out a pile of colorful ribbons. "You'll be safe in here," she told me. Golden-Miranda brought me a little cup of water to drink. Nice.

"This is strictly against the rules," Mrs. Wright insisted. "I demand an explanation!"

"Yes, please tell us what happened, Richie," Mrs. Brisbane said in a VERY-VERY-VERY mad voice.

"I can't believe Humphrey was on board," he said. "How'd he get there?"

That was a question only *I* could answer.

"We'll figure that out," Mrs. Brisbane said. "But why did you sink your own ship?"

"I didn't mean to sink it!" Richie protested, and I believed him. "I just wanted to show Kirk I know about boats, too."

Mrs. Brisbane turned to Kirk. "Do you know what he means?"

Kirk shrugged. "Um, I guess he didn't think I let him help enough."

"You didn't let me help at all!" Richie said. What he said was true.

Mrs. Brisbane turned to Kirk again. "Why didn't you let Richie help?"

Kirk, who was always cracking jokes, looked very serious. "I wanted to win. I thought we had a better chance if I did the work."

"So whose fault was it that Humphrey almost drowned?" the teacher asked.

Whoa! Hearing her say that made me shake and quake.

"Mine," Richie answered. "But I wouldn't want anything to happen to Humphrey."

"It was your fault, Richie." Mrs. Brisbane nodded. "Don't you agree, Kirk?"

Kirk stared at the ground and didn't answer right away. Finally he said, "Yes, but I guess it was kind of my fault, too, because I made Richie mad. Winning wouldn't have been worth it if something had happened to Humphrey. I'm sorry."

"Well, don't apologize to me!" Mrs. Brisbane said. She sounded pretty upset.

Kirk looked at Richie. "Sorry, Richie. I wasn't very nice to you."

"I'm sorry, too." Richie looked embarrassed. "It was a dumb idea to bring the submarine. I just was so mad."

"The next thing I want to know is who put Humphrey in the boat," Mrs. Brisbane said. "But I'll deal with that later. Right now, it's time for our treasure hunt!"

My classmates and I squealed with delight when Mr. Brisbane passed out treasure maps. (My guess about *trea* from the list was right.) He said, "Boys and girls, it's said that the famous pirate Captain Kidd buried his treasure right here by Potter's Pond."

So that's who the captain was: Captain Kidd!

"Follow these old maps to find the hidden treasure," Mr. Brisbane explained. "Remember, *X* marks the spot."

My friends set off among the paths and trees, looking for clues. I longed to join them, but I'd had enough adventures for one day, so I watched and listened.

It wasn't too long before I heard Mandy shout, "I found it! The *X* is right here!"

There was a rush of footsteps. Mrs. Brisbane picked up my basket and said, "Come on, Humphrey. You might as well see this, too."

She carried me to a little clearing where Mandy, Art and Tabitha stood by an old trunk that looked just like a pirate's treasure chest with a big *X* carved on top. She pushed my lid back so I could see better.

"Should we open it?" Tabitha asked.

They all agreed they should, but just as they tipped the lid open, one-two-three pirates leaped out of the bushes!

My friends screamed at the sight of the strangers, who lunged at the crowd. My heart just about jumped out of my chest. I'd almost forgotten about the pirates!

"Arrgh!" growled the first pirate.

"Avast," snarled the second pirate.

The third pirate was even more menacing. "Stop right there, mateys," he roared. "Don't even be thinking of touching Captain Kidd's treasure!"

The three pirates stood in front of the treasure chest, looking SCARY-SCARY-SCARY and MEAN-MEAN-MEAN.

The first pirate had on a bright red shirt and a bright blue sash. He had dark hair, a big gold earring and a patch over one eye.

The second pirate wore shiny black pants, a long red coat with big gold buttons and a genuine pirate hat! (At least it looked genuine to me.) He also had big round glasses. Funny, I'd never seen a pirate with glasses before.

The third pirate had striped pants tucked into black boots, a black tunic with a belt, a kerchief on his head and a big black mustache.

"Landlubbers!" he shouted in a familiar voice. "Back off from me treasure or I'll introduce ye to Davy Jones!"

My friends screamed and backed up. But I could swear I'd seen that mustache before.

Suddenly Richie called out, "It's Uncle Aldo!" and the other students started to laugh and shriek.

"It's Aldo!" they yelled.

Of course, it was Aldo! He'd been practicing being a pirate for weeks. He gave a jolly laugh when they recognized him.

But what about the others? The first pirate pushed up his eye patch and we could see who he was: Principal Morales.

"Arrgh!" he repeated, but this time he was smiling.

My friends all squealed with laughter.

The second pirate took off his hat and bowed before us. "Greetings," he said, and we all realized that he was Mr. Fitch. That pirate hat in the library was his after all.

Suddenly, these pirates didn't seem scary at all!

"Be ye ready to unlock the secrets of the deep?" asked Aldo as he opened the lid. Inside were mounds of yummy sandwiches and juices and cookies.

My friends acted as if they'd never seen food before. They screamed with delight as they hurried toward the chest.

Seth and Tabitha got there first, but as soon as they put their hands on the food, another voice rang out.

"How dare ye touch me treasure?" This was definitely a female voice. "Stop or the lot of ye will end up asleep in the deep!"

Everyone gasped—including me—as out of the

bushes stepped a *female* pirate. She had on tall boots, a red skirt, big gold hoop earrings and a white top with billowy sleeves.

Even with the pirate hat and the eye patch she wore, I could see her bouncy black curls. And I knew that voice!

"That treasure came all the way from Brazil . . . " she started. But my friends didn't let her finish.

"Ms. Mac! Ms. Mac!" they shouted with joy as they rushed forward to greet her.

There she was: Ms. Mac, the teacher who rescued me from Pet-O-Rama, who gave me a notebook and pencil and first discovered what a handsome and smart hamster I am.

"Ms. Mac is back!" I squeaked loudly, surprising even myself.

Ms. Mac hurried over to my basket. "Humphrey!" she cried. "There's the real treasure."

She gently scratched my back, and I had a FUNNY-FUNNY-FUNNY feeling from the wiggly tip of my nose to the squiggly tips of my toes.

I'd had that feeling before, way back when.

I think they call it love.

‿◡‿

All of my friends loved Ms. Mac and wanted to be near her. They gave her sandwiches and juice and gathered around her.

"What do you think of our secret guest?" Mrs. Brisbane asked us.

Ms. Mac was our secret guest! So that's what the *secret g* on the list stood for!

"Do you have to go back to Brazil?" Miranda asked.

"No, my term ended," Ms. Mac explained. "I'm back here to stay—if I can find a job."

While everyone ate, Mr. Fitch played the harmonica and Aldo and Mr. Morales danced the sailor's hornpipe. (Aldo did a better job, but he'd had a lot of practice.)

"Well done, me hearties!" I squeaked, but no one could hear me over the applause.

Then Mrs. Brisbane quieted everyone down. "Don't you think it's time for the prizes?"

In her hand were the ribbons she'd taken out of the basket.

Everyone cheered when Sayeh and Miranda received blue ribbons. Even though their swan boat didn't last, it definitely was the Most Beautiful Boat.

But when it came to the Most Seaworthy Boat, it wasn't so easy to decide who won.

"Undoubtedly, the tall ship would have won," Mr. Brisbane said. "But because of what happened, I can only award it honorable mention." Richie and Kirk didn't seem disappointed to receive red ribbons.

"As for first place, we were all so busy worrying about Humphrey, no one really noticed which boat came in first. Since Seth and Tabitha's Chinese junk and Heidi and Gail's sailboat both made it to shore, we're calling it a tie. You'll all receive gold ribbons."

From the cheers and smiles, I could tell that no one

was disappointed. Seth and Tabitha did a funny victory dance. Heidi and Gail joined in.

Then Mrs. Morgenstern came over to congratulate the girls. "You did a great job!" she said. "I was so focused on you winning the Most Beautiful award, I didn't think of you actually winning the race. But you did it!"

Gail and Heidi beamed.

"And the sail was spectacular! That white sail on the blue water—it was a classic. Gail, you were right all along. I'm very proud of you."

Gail and her mom hugged. Then Heidi and Gail's mom hugged. Then Heidi and Gail hugged. I wished there was someone for me to hug, although hugging might be a little dangerous for a small hamster.

It was almost time to get back to school. As everyone else was busy packing up, I spotted Kirk and Richie wading into the water to retrieve their tall ship, which was half submerged near the edge of the pond. Luckily, the water only came up to their knees. Sayeh and Miranda watched onshore as a few of their colorful feathers floated by. Garth and A.J. looked for their boat, too, but all they could find was the flag. Art and Mandy waded in the water, but the Viking ship was totally gone.

On the edge of the pond, Mr. Morales cupped his hands around his mouth and yelled, "If you see an old raft down there, let me know!"

When Kirk and Richie finally pulled the remains of the tall ship out of the water, it was muddy and mucky, but they cleaned it up, working together.

I was happy to stay in my basket on the bus ride back. I sat between Mrs. Brisbane and Ms. Mac—the best seat in the house. If I grabbed onto the inside of the basket, I could lift the top with my head just enough to see them both.

"You certainly picked an interesting day to return," Mrs. Brisbane said.

"Every day is interesting for the kids in Room Twenty-six," Ms. Mac replied.

Mrs. Brisbane reached in her jacket and pulled out a piece of paper. "In all the excitement, I forgot to check my list."

Ms. Mac and I could both see it.

lunches and drinks (in chest)
treasure maps
Captain Kidd and his motley crew
blue, red, gold ribbons for prizes
secret guest: Ms. Mac

"You didn't forget anything," Ms. Mac said.

Mrs. Brisbane folded up her paper. "No, but a few things happened that weren't on the list. You know what they say: the best-laid plans of mice and men often go astray."

The best-laid Plans of hamsters go astray, too. But that's what makes life interesting.

Soon, Mrs. Wright led us all in singing a boat song

that was very interesting because different groups started it and ended it at different times. I squeaked up the loudest of all.

> Row, row, row your boat
> Gently down the stream.
> Merrily, merrily, merrily, merrily,
> Life is but a dream.

It was a fun song to sing, and I thought, maybe someday I'd like to row *gently* down a stream. Even though today's trip had almost turned into a nightmare, seeing Ms. Mac again was definitely a dream come true.

A good heart, mateys: there be the only treasure worth having!

FROM JOLLY ROGER'S GUIDE TO LIFE,
by I.C. Waters

Land Ho!

When we got back to Room 26, I was almost too tired to squeak, but I managed to tell Og I'd had a great adventure, nearly drowned, but lived to tell the tale.

"BOING!" At least he sounded interested.

I didn't get to tell him more because the bell rang for recess and my classmates streamed out of the room. The room wasn't empty for long, though, because Mrs. Wright, Mr. Morales and Ms. Mac all joined Mrs. Brisbane in the classroom.

"Do you have a minute, Sue?" the principal asked. He was still wearing his red shirt with the bright blue sash. He'd taken off his earring and eye patch, though.

"Of course," she said. "Please sit down."

It's always funny to see grown-ups sitting on the kid-size chairs in the classroom. I tried to imagine them as students. Mr. Morales would be a good student with a playful streak. Mrs. Brisbane would be an excellent student, like Sayeh. Of course, Ms. Mac would be an almost perfect human, like Miranda.

But try as I did, I couldn't imagine Mrs. Wright as a child.

"Did any of the students admit to smuggling Humphrey on the boat?" Mr. Morales asked.

Mrs. Brisbane shook her head. "No. I think Kirk and Richie felt so terrible, they would have confessed to it. But they didn't."

"Maybe someone was jealous of their boat and did it to get them into trouble," Mrs. Wright suggested.

"Maybe," said Mrs. Brisbane. "But I just can't imagine any of my students doing that."

Mrs. Wright sniffed loudly. "I know you think all your students are perfect," she said. "But someone had to do it. He certainly couldn't have gotten there all by himself."

Suddenly, everyone turned to look at me.

"I didn't plan on going along," I squeaked in self-defense. "It just happened."

Ms. Mac laughed her lovely, tinkling laugh.

"He's been known to get out of his cage before," Mrs. Brisbane said. "But Bert fixed the door so he can't get out."

Mrs. Wright stood up and clomped over to my cage. "Even if he could open the cage, you can't tell me this little rat or guinea pig or whatever he is could possibly get down from the table, run all across the room and get in the boat by himself. Impossible! Simply impossible!"

"I'm a hamster!" I squeaked back at her. "And it's NOT-NOT-NOT impossible!"

112

"BOING-BOING-BOING!" Og chimed in.

This time everyone laughed, except Mrs. Wright.

I guess Mr. Morales was sorry he'd laughed. "You have a point, Ruth."

Mrs. Wright sniffed again. Maybe she was allergic to hamsters. "We can't have animals running willy-nilly around the school and the buses and on picnics."

"It was only one animal," Mrs. Brisbane said softly.

The bell rang again, and Mr. Morales stood up. "Look, Mrs. Brisbane has been handling her students and their problems for thirty years. I think she can handle this one. Let's move on."

He left, along with Ms. Mac and Mrs. Wright. Just before my friends returned from recess, Mrs. Brisbane came over to my cage and jiggled the door. It was fastened tightly, of course.

"Humphrey, I must say, life is never dull with you around."

"Thanks," I squeaked. "That's what a classroom hamster is for."

⋅∽⋅

After school, when we were alone, I told Og the whole story. When I finished, I remembered something else.

"I have to say, Og, that as I was about to sink, I thought of you." It was strange to remember seeing his goofy face flash before me.

"I know if you'd been there, you would have saved me because you can swim. And because you're my friend."

I was surprised at how quickly Og responded with a BOING-BOING-BOING-BOING-BOING!

"I'd do the same for you," I continued. "I can't swim, but I'd think of something. I guess we make a pretty good team after all. Maybe Kirk and Richie will, too."

Og dived into the water with an impressive splash.

And with that, I crawled into my sleeping hut and slept soundly, dreaming about the high seas, pirates, best friends and yes, Ms. Mac.

No more boat building. No more pirate talk. No more contests. The very next day, we were back to regular old school again, but after my close call with Davy Jones's locker, I didn't mind.

Not that the subject of the boat race didn't come up. Mrs. Brisbane began the day with a very serious look on her face. "Boys and girls, we still don't know who sneaked Humphrey into that boat and onto the bus. If the guilty party would like to confess now, it would make all our lives a little easier."

There were some shuffling feet and a few cleared throats, but no one confessed. There was no one *to* confess, except for me.

"I hate to punish the whole class . . ." Mrs. Brisbane began.

I couldn't take it any longer. "I did it! It was ME-ME-ME!" I squeaked as loudly as I could.

Everyone laughed. Even Mrs. Brisbane.

"I guess Humphrey has the last word for now," she said. "If anyone would like to confess to me in private, I'd appreciate it. Meanwhile, we're moving on."

Over the next few days, there were a few changes in Room 26.

First of all, Richie and Kirk had to write letters of apology to each other. Then each of them had to give a speech to the class, apologizing for almost ruining the boat race.

In his speech, Kirk said that teamwork was more important than winning and the team that works together always comes out ahead in the end. As usual, he ended with a joke. This time, it was one I'd already heard, about the scarecrow winning the award for being outstanding in his field.

Richie made the point that two wrongs don't make a *right*. At first I thought he was talking about *Mrs. Wright,* and I shivered a little just thinking about her whistle, though she's a very good song leader.

But then I realized that he meant just because Kirk treated Richie the wrong way didn't make it right for Richie to break the rules and bring along the submarine.

I cheered loudly for both speeches.

Aldo changed back to his regular non-pirate ways of talking and cleaning, thank goodness. But every once in a while, he'd do a little hornpipe dance while he was dusting.

The other change in Room 26 was something—or someone—wonderful. Ms. Mac came in to help Mrs.

Brisbane for two hours every day. Then she would go to the library and help Mr. Fitch for another hour or two.

She smelled so good, and she always remembered to bring me yummy treats like apple slices and strawberries. Having her around was a dream come true.

One day, she asked Mrs. Brisbane if she could have lunch with her. They sat across from each other at Mrs. Brisbane's desk and took out sandwiches and water and yummy-looking fruit and they talked.

"I'm so glad it worked out with Humphrey," Ms. Mac said. "When I left here, I wasn't sure you'd like having a classroom hamster."

"I wasn't sure myself," Mrs. Brisbane admitted. "But he's added a lot to the class."

"Good," said Ms. Mac. She chewed on her sandwich a little more and then said, "I'm a little worried about what I'm going to do now that I'm back. I need to make some money."

"Funny, I've been worrying about that, too," Mrs. Brisbane replied. She didn't look worried, though. In fact, she was grinning. "And I have some ideas."

Ms. Mac's big brown eyes got even bigger. "What?"

"I don't want to say yet, but you are a very talented young teacher, and I know of several opportunities coming up." Mrs. Brisbane was being awfully mysterious. "You'll find out soon."

"WHAT-WHAT-WHAT?" I shouted.

The two women chuckled. "It sounds like Humphrey has a few ideas, too," Ms. Mac said.

"He always does," Mrs. Brisbane agreed.

"Speaking of Humphrey, has anyone confessed to smuggling him into the boat?"

"Well, yes. You actually heard him confess." So Mrs. Brisbane had understood me!!

Ms. Mac glanced over at my cage. "Could Humphrey really do that?"

Mrs. Brisbane looked my way, too. "If there's one thing I've learned this year, when it comes to Humphrey, *anything* is possible."

"BOING-BOING!" Og twanged, splashing in his tank.

The two teachers burst out laughing.

When they finished their lunches, they each gave me a treat. From Mrs. Brisbane, it was a small and crunchy carrot. From Ms. Mac, it was a soft, sweet slice of banana.

I crossed my paws and hoped they have lunch in Room 26 more often!

～•～

And then something really wonderful happened. Ms. Mac brought Mr. Fitch to Room 26 one day. He said that due to my bravery during the boat race and my contributions to the class, he was presenting me with my very own library card!

And there it was: a lovely little rectangle that read, *This card grants full library privileges at Longfellow School to HUMPHREY.* He taped it to the outside of my cage.

Everyone applauded. Then Miranda Golden, my special friend, raised her hand. "But how is Humphrey going to check out books? He can't get to the library by himself!"

Oh, humans! There's so much they don't know. In fact, I was already planning to stroll down to the library later that night to see if there was a good movie I could watch.

"We'll just have to help him out," Mrs. Brisbane answered. "Just like he's always helped us."

"Hooray for Humphrey Dumpty!" A.J. suddenly shouted. My friends all joined in, and I even heard Og say, "BOING!" in agreement.

"Thanks, mateys," I squeaked back happily. "HOORAY-HOORAY-HOORAY!"

Even a pirate can say thank ye, mateys!
From JOLLY ROGER'S GUIDE TO LIFE.
by I.C. Waters

Humphrey's List of Ten Things You Should Know About Pirates

1. Many pirates wore earrings, not just for looks, but because they thought it made their eyesight better.
2. "Going to Davy Jones's locker" means losing your life at sea.
3. Although Long John Silver kept a parrot as a pet, most pirates probably didn't have parrots. Dogs and cats were often on sailing ships to help keep down the rodent population. (As a rodent, let me tell you that dogs and cats are VERY-VERY-VERY scary.)
4. Food on pirate ships wasn't very good. Pirates lived mostly on hard biscuits and a little meat. Sometimes they brought fruit like limes on board to prevent a disease called scurvy.
5. There were some famous female pirates, like Anne Bonny and Mary Read. (Ms. Mac was not one of them. She's much too nice to be a pirate.)
6. A "piece of eight" was a silver coin that was worth eight of the Spanish coin called the *Real*. Really! A "doubloon" was a gold coin.
7. A "landlubber" is someone who doesn't know how to sail. I used to be a landlubber, but not anymore!

8. A pirate says, "Thar she blows," when a whale is spotted.

9. The poop deck of a ship is the part farthest in the back, above the captain's quarters. It does not have anything to do with poo!

10. While it's fun to talk and dress and pretend to be a pirate, they are not nice humans. Yes, there are still pirates today, so beware, me hearties!

Oh, and yes, there really is a book called *Treasure Island* with Long John Silver and Jim Hawkins in it. It's by Robert Louis Stevenson, and you can find it in your library. If you don't have a card, get one!

Ahoy, matey!

Humphrey may only be a small hamster, but when it comes to adventure, Humphrey's ideas are BIG-BIG-BIG! He's already had many exciting escapades outside of his cage, but in *Adventure According to Humphrey*, he gets carried away and *almost* ends up over his furry little head. Eek!

Despite his previous encounters with fierce creatures such as cats and dogs, and other exciting (and dangerous) exploits, Humphrey still longs to have the kind of adventures his human classmates do.

When Mrs. Brisbane announces that the class will build their own model boats and then try them out on Potter's Pond, Humphrey's head is filled with thoughts of sailing—even though he knows it's unsqueakably dangerous for hamsters to get wet. Even though he knows he'll be left behind on sailing day, while his friends design their pirate vessels and tall ships, he sketches his ideal boat, the *SS Golden Hamster*, in his notebook. At least a hamster can dream!

I spend a lot of time traveling to schools and libraries, and one day it occurred to me that Humphrey had done a lot of wonderful things at Longfellow School, but he had never been to the library! How could I have left out something so important? I have always been a big fan of the library, starting with the little bookmobile where I got all my favorite books when I was a child.

So in this book, Humphrey not only goes to the library with his class, but he also finds a way to sneak back in night after night to watch a video of *Treasure Island* and to stare at the awesome fish tank with the tiny shipwreck at the bottom.

At the same time, Mrs. Brisbane reads a rollicking pirate book to the class; Aldo starts to talk and act like a pirate; *and* there's a mysterious pirate hat hidden in the library. How can Humphrey help but think about pirates?

Humphrey has more to deal with than just dreams of adventure. He's busy helping solve a misunderstanding between Gail and her mom, who is helping with the boat building. And Richie has a BIG-BIG-BIG problem with his friend Kirk that only Humphrey understands. But can he stop Richie from making a very bad—even dangerous— decision?

Then there's the mysterious party Mrs. Brisbane is planning. Humphrey's brain spins as fast as his hamster wheel as he tries to figure out what she's got in mind.

Nothing Humphrey can imagine prepares him for the biggest—and most dangerous—adventure of his life as he sets sail on a tall ship on Potter's Pond. And he certainly could never imagine the amazing, wonderful, marvelous, unexpected surprise waiting for him on the other shore! (I think you'll like it, too.)

So set sail for adventure. And if you don't already have one, go to your local community library and get your own library card. (It's free.) There are hundreds of exciting adventures just waiting for you, right there on those beautiful shelves of books!

YO-HO-HO!

Betty G. Birney

Meet Humphrey!

Everyone's favorite classroom pet!

Want more FUN-FUN-FUN?

Find fun Humphrey activities and teachers' guides at www.penguin.com/humphrey.

Learn more about Betty G. Birney and Humphrey at www.bettybirney.com.

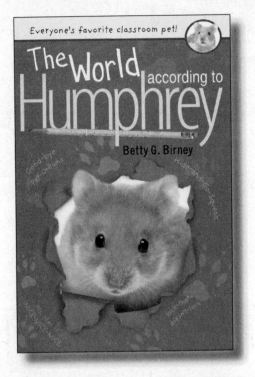

Welcome to Room 26, Humphrey!

You can learn a lot about life by observing another species. That's what Humphrey was told when he was first brought to Room 26. And boy, is it true! In addition to his classroom escapades, each weekend this amazing hamster gets to sleep over with a different student. Soon Humphrey learns to read, write, and even shoot rubber bands (only in self-defense). Humphrey's life would be perfect, if only the teacher weren't out to get him!

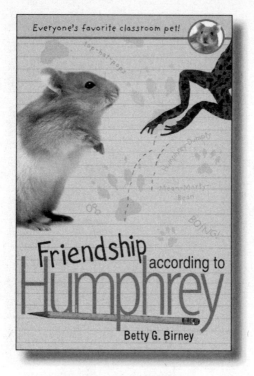

Everyone's favorite classroom pet!

Friendship according to Humphrey

Betty G. Birney

A New Friend?

Room 26 has a new class pet, Og the frog. Humphrey can't wait to be friends with Og, but Og doesn't seem interested. To make matters worse, the students are so fascinated by Og, they almost stop paying attention to Humphrey altogether! Humphrey knows that friendship can be tricky business, but if any hamster can become buddies with a frog, Humphrey can!

Humphrey to the Rescue!

Humphrey the hamster loves to solve problems for his classmates in Room 26, but he never meant to create one! Golden-Miranda, one of his favorite students, gets blamed when Humphrey is caught outside of his cage while she's in charge. Since no one knows about his lock-that-doesn't-lock, he can't exactly squeak up to defend her. Can Humphrey clear Miranda's name without giving up his freedom forever?

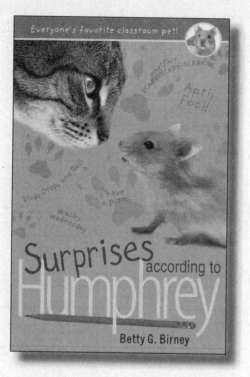

Surprises for Humphrey!

A classroom hamster has to be ready for anything, but suddenly there are LOTS-LOTS-LOTS of big surprises in Humphrey's world. Some are exciting, such as a new hamster ball. But some are scary, such as a run-in with a cat and a new janitor who might be from another planet. Even with all that's going on, Humphrey finds time to help his classmates with their problems. But will Mrs. Brisbane's unsqueakable surprise be too much for Humphrey to handle?

Everyone's favorite classroom pet!

Adventure according to Humphrey

Betty G. Birney

AHOY, MATEY!

Humphrey Sets Sail!

Humphrey's friends in Room 26 are learning about the ocean and boats, and Humphrey can't contain his excitement. He dreams about being a pirate on the high seas; and when the students build miniature boats to sail on Potter's Pond, Humphrey thinks he might get his wish. But trouble with the boats puts Humphrey in a sea of danger. Will Humphrey squeak his way out of the biggest adventure of his life?

Everyone's favorite classroom pet!

The Haunted Howler   Camp is FUN-FUN-FUN!

The great outdoors

CAMP HAPPY HOLLOW

Owoooo!   SCRITCH-SCRITCH-SCRITCH   SQUEAK-SQUEAK-SQUEAK

Summer according to **Humphrey**

Betty G. Birney

Humphrey Is a Happy Camper!

When Humphrey hears that school is ending, he can't believe his ears. What's a classroom hamster to do if there's no more school? It turns out that Mrs. Brisbane has planned something thrilling for Humphrey and Og the frog: they're going to camp with Ms. Mac and lots of the kids from Room 26! Camp is full of FUN-FUN-FUN new experiences, but it's also a little scary. Humphrey is always curious about new adventures, but could camp be too wild even for him?

Everyone's favorite classroom pet!

School Days according to **Humphrey**

Betty G. Birney

Who Are These Kids?!

After an unsqueakably fun summer at camp, Humphrey can't wait to get back to Room 26 and see all of his class-mates. But something fur-raising happens on the first day of school—some kids he's never seen before come into Mrs. Brisbane's room. And she doesn't even tell them they're in the wrong room! While Humphrey gets to know the new students, he wonders about his old friends. Where could they be? What could have hap-pened to them?! It's a big mystery for a small hamster to solve. But as always, Humphrey will find a way!

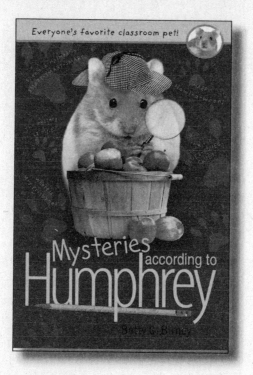

Mysteries according to
Humphrey

Betty G. Birney

EEK-EEK-EEK! Mrs. Brisbane Is Missing!

Humphrey has always investigated things, like why Speak-Up-Sayeh was so quiet and Tall-Paul and Small-Paul didn't get along, but this is a true mystery—Mrs. Brisbane is missing! She just didn't show up in Room 26 one morning and no one told Humphrey why. The class has a substitute teacher, called Mr. E., but he's no Mrs. Brisbane. Humphrey has just learned about Sherlock Holmes, so he vows to be just as SMART-SMART-SMART about collecting clues and following leads to solve the mystery of Mrs. Brisbane. . . .

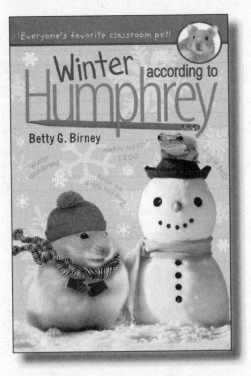

Everyone's favorite classroom pet!

Winter according to Humphrey

Betty G. Birney

A Hamsterific Celebration
of the Best Time of the Year!

Room 26 is abuzz. The students are making costumes
and practicing their special songs for the Winter Wonder-
land program, and Humphrey is fascinated by all the
ways his classmates celebrate the holidays (especially
the yummy food). He also has problems to solve like
how to get Do-It-Now-Daniel to stop procrastinating,
convince Helpful-Holly to stop stressing over presents,
and come up with the perfect gift for Og the frog. Of
course he manages to do all that while adding delightful
heart and humor to the holiday season.

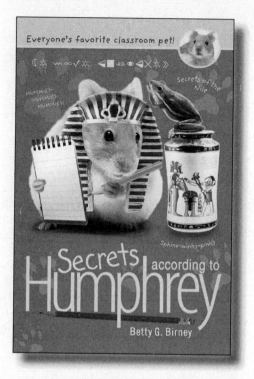

Everyone's favorite classroom pet!

Secrets of the Nile

MUMMIES-
MUMMIES-
MUMMIES!

Sphinx-winks-pinks

Secrets according to Humphrey

Betty G. Birney

Room 26 Is Full of Secrets, and Humphrey Doesn't Like It One Bit!

So many secrets are flying around Room 26 that Humphrey can barely keep track. Mrs. Brisbane knows a student is leaving, but Humphrey can't figure out which one. (Even more confusing, Mrs. Brisbane seems unsqueakably *happy* about it.) The class is studying the Ancient Egyptians, and some of the kids have made up secret clubs and secret codes. Even Aldo is holding back news from Humphrey.

Humphrey's job as classroom pet is to help his humans solve their problems, but all these secrets are making it HARD-HARD-HARD!

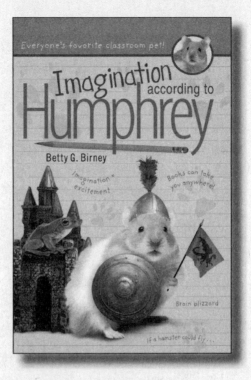

Everyone's favorite classroom pet!

Imagination according to Humphrey

Betty G. Birney

Imagination excitement

Books can take you anywhere!

Brain blizzard

If a hamster could fly...

Even a Little Hamster Can Have a Big Imagination!

Imaginations are running wild in Mrs. Brisbane's class, but Humphrey is stumped. His friends are writing about where they would go if they could fly, but Humphrey is HAPPY-HAPPY-HAPPY right where he is in Room 26. It's pawsitively easy for Humphrey to picture exciting adventures with dragons and knights in the story Mrs. Brisbane is reading aloud. If only his imagination wouldn't disappear when he tries to write. Luckily, Humphrey likes a challenge, and Mrs. Brisbane has lots of writing tips that do the trick.

WATCH OUT FOR HUMPHREY'S
BOOK OF UNSQUEAKABLY
FUN JOKES AND PUZZLES!

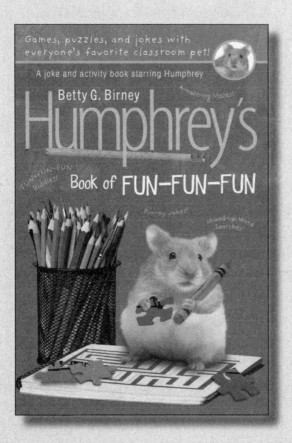

IF YOU LIKE PETS AND ANIMALS,
BE SURE TO PICK UP HUMPHREY'S
BOOK OF PET FACTS AND TIPS!